Fresh Apples

Rachel Trezise was born in the Rhondda Valley in 1978. She studied at Glamorgan and Limerick Universities. Her novel *In and Out of the Goldfish Bowl* won a place on the Orange Futures List in 2002. *Harpers & Queen* magazine voted her New Face of Literature, 2003. She is a freelance music and arts journalist, currently working on her second novel, as well as a documentary about Welsh rock music. She still lives in the Rhondda. *Fresh Apples* is her first short fiction collection.

Rachel Trezise is the first writer of her generation to explore the territory of Welsh drug culture and poverty, and at the same time be laugh-out-loud funny. She's a great comedian.
Peter Florence – **Harpers & Queen**

For Darran

Contents

'Oh, isn't life a terrible thing, thank God?'
Dylan Thomas – *Under Milk Wood*

Fresh Apples

When you get oil from a locomotive engine all over the arse
of your best blue jeans, it looks like shit: black and sticky.
I can see it's black, even in the dark. I stand on the sty
and try to brush it away with the back of my hand, bent
awkward over the fence, but it sticks to my skin, and then
there's nowhere to wipe my hands. Laugh, they would –
Rhys Davies and Kristian – if they could see me now. Don't
know why I wore my best stuff. 'Wear clean knickers,' my
mother'd say, 'in case you have an accident.' She'd say
knickers even when she meant pants. She's a feminist, see.
But it's not like anyone would notice if I was wearing pants
or not. Johnny Mental from up the street, he said when he
was at school the police would pay him at the end of the
day to look for bits of fingers and bits of intestines here,
before he went home for tea. If it can do that, if it can slice

your tubes like green beans, who's going to notice if you had skid marks in your kecks? I can still hear the train chugging away, or perhaps it's my imagination. Over in the town I can hear drunk people singing but closer, I can hear cicadas – that noise you think only exists in American films to show you that something horrific is about to happen – it's real. It's hot too. Even in the night it's still hot and I'm panting like a dog. I'm sure it's this weather that's making me fucking nuts. I'm alive anyway; I can feel my blood pumping so it's all been a waste of time. Forget it now, that's the thing to do. Oh, you want to know about it, of course you do. Nosy bastard you are. Well I'll tell you and then I'll forget it, and you can forget it too. And just remember this: I'm not proud of it. Let's get that straight from the outset. The whole thing is a bloody encumbrance. (New word that, encumbrance. I found it in my father's things this morning.)

Thursday night it started, but the summer has been going on forever, for years it seems like, the sun visors down on the café and fruiterer's in town, the smell of barbecued food wafting on the air, and never going away. And the smell of mountain fires, of timber crumbling and being swallowed by a rolling wave of orange flames. On the Bwlch we were, at the entrance of the forestry. There used to be a climbing frame and a set of swings made from the logs from the trees. It's gone now but we still go there, us and the car and van shaggers. Sitting on a picnic table with my legs hanging over the edge so I could see down Holly's top when she leaned forward on the bench, her coffee colour skin going into two perfect, hard spheres, like snooker balls, or drawer knobs, poking the cartoon on her T-shirt out at either side. She was drinking blackcurrant, the plastic bottle to her mouth, the purple liquid inside it swishing back and fore. I asked her for some. I wouldn't normally – I'm shy, I'd lose my tongue, but my mouth was dry and scratchy from the sun. Yes, she said, but when I gave the bottle back she wiped the rim on the hem of her skirt like I had AIDs. Kristian and Rhys Davies John Davies, they had handfuls of stone chippings, throwing them at Escorts when they went past, their techno music jumping. Jealous they are, of the cars and the stereos but fuck that dance music, it's Metallica for me. (Don't tell them that.) It's his real name by the way, Rhys Davies John Davies: the first part after some gay Welsh poet, the second after his armed-robber father, shacked up in Swansea prison.

Every time something passed us, a lorry or a motorbike, it grated on the cattle grid in the road. That's how Kristian came up with the cow tipping idea. Only we couldn't go cow tipping because you can only tip cows when they're sleeping, in the middle of the night and it'd take ten of us to move one, so Holly had to go one better.

'Let's go and start a fire!' she said.

'Don't be stupid,' I said. 'We should be proud of this mountain, Hol. They haven't got mountains like this in England. And you'll kill all the nature.'

'Nature!?' she said. She rolled her eyes at Jaime and Angharad. 'It's not the fuckin' Amazonian rain forest, Matt,' she said. She can be a cow when she wants, see. 'C'mon girls,' she said and she flicked her curly hair out of her face. 'When there's a fire, what else is there?'

'A fire engine?' Jaime said.

'Exactly. Firemen. Proper men!' And she started up off into the trees, shaking her tiny denim arse at us. The girls followed her and then the boys followed the girls. So that just left me. And Sarah.

Sarah, Jaime's cerebral palsy kid sister. She's not abnormal or ugly, just a little bit fat, and she rocks back and fore slightly, and she has a spasm in her hand that makes her look like she's doing something sexual to herself all the time. But she's brighter than Jaime gives her credit for, even when she's got that big, green chewing gum bubble coming out of her mouth and hiding her whole face. I just never knew what to say to her – how to start a conversation. I smiled at her clumsily and tried to giggle at the silence. We stayed like that, her sitting on her hands, chewing her gum loudly so I could hear her saliva swish around in her mouth, until a fireman came with thick, black stubble over his face, fanning the burning ferns out with a giant fly squat because he couldn't get his engine up onto the mountain.

'Come and get me you sexy fucker,' Holly was shouting at him, hiding her face behind a tree. That's when I went home.

On Friday morning, on the portable TV in the kitchen there was an appeal from Rhymney Valley Fire Service for kids to stop setting fire to the mountains. 'Nine times out of ten it's arson,' the man's voice boomed. 'It's children with matches.' The volume's broke, see, either it has to be on full, or it has to be on mute.

'That's kids, is it?' my mother said, hanging over the

draining board, a red gingham cloth stuffed into a tall, transparent cylinder. 'I always thought it was bits of glass left in the ground starting it. It can happen like that when it's hot can't it?' My father ignored her, standing at arm's length from the frying pan, turning sausages over with his chef's tongs. She gave up pushing the cloth down into the glass and washed the bubbles out under the cold tap. I watched the rest of the announcement, spooning Coco Pops into my mouth, the milk around them yellowy and sweet.

'The mountains are tinder dry,' the man said, 'so please don't go near them with matches. While we're attending to an arson attack there could be a serious house fire in the town.' I remembered the look of helplessness on the fireman's face while he sweated over the ferns, Holly asking him to fuck her. He knew that as soon as he'd gone we'd start it again so he'd have to come back, sweating again. I opened one of the blue cover English exercise books my father was marking at the kitchen table before he got up to cook breakfast, and I read some kid's modern version of *Hamlet*. Crap it was, but I found two new words, *psychodrama* and *necromancy*.

Later, at Rhys Davies' house, his mother was still cleaning spew off plastic beer-garden tables, and his father was still in jail, so Kristian and Rhys, they were drinking a box of cheap red wine.

'Matt,' Kristian said, dropping the Playstation pad on the carpet. 'Holly got her tits out last night.'

'No she fuckin' didn't,' I said.

'She fuckin' did and you missed it,' he said.

'No she didn't,' Rhys said.

They offered me the wine but I didn't want it. I went to the kitchen and scoured it for Mrs Davies' chocolate. She had a shit load hidden from Rhys' sister in Mr Davies' old lunch box, under the basket-weave cutlery tray.

'I wouldn't poke 'er anyway,' Kristian was saying when I went back. 'She's a snobby bitch. She's the only form five girl I haven't poked and I don't want to poke 'er. She's frigid, inshee?'

I didn't know what frigid meant but I made a note in my head to find out and another one to remember to poke some girl before people started to think I was gay.

'Imagine all the new girls when we start tech!' Kristian said. We were starting tech in a month. Kristian wanted to be a plumber. His father told him, with some prison guard standing nearby, that he'd always have money if he was a plumber. Strange, because Mr Davies was a plumber but he tried to rob an all-night garage with a stick in a black bag. Kristian and me, we were doing a bricklaying NVQ because the careers teacher said it was a good course.

'The girls from the church school'll be starting the same time and none of them 'ave got pinhole pussies,' Kristian said. 'Johnny Mental told me, they're all slags.'

I was leaning out of the window watching the elderly woman next door feeding lettuce to her tortoise. It was still really hot but she was wearing a cream colour Aran cardigan. I was wondering if there was a job somewhere which involved collecting words to put into a dictionary or something, or a course which taught you to play drums like Tommy Lee so I could throw sticks into the air after a roll and catch them in my teeth because I didn't find bricks and girls with big fannies that exciting. I unwrapped the chocolate but it had already melted.

That night we were on the mountain again, standing on the roof of the old brick caretaker's hut, looking down into town at the small groups of women walking like matchstick people to the pubs in their sunburn, their too tight trousers and gold strap sandals, the men in blue jeans and ironed shirts. Holly, Angharad and Jaime, they came up via the new road because they had Holly's collie dog on a lead. There's a farm across the road, see, with a sheepdog in the field, a white one with black patches around its eyes like a canine panda. It barks at the sight of another dog and keeps barking until the farmer comes over and tells us to fuck off before he shoots us. He thinks anyone under the age of eighteen is committing some heinous crime just by breathing. So we missed looking down into Holly's cheesecloth blouse as she passed underneath us. Sarah was five minutes behind them, wobbling over the banking, her thick white shins shining, her short yellow hair bouncing on her fat, pink head. There was some kind of in joke going on with Kristian and Rhys and Angharad and Holly and Jaime. They all seemed to be winking at one another, or talking to one another but with no words coming out of their mouths. I thought I caught Kristian doing a wanker signal behind my back but I passed it off as a hallucination, with the sun being so fucking hot. Then the dog began to cough.

'Holly, there's something wrong with your dog,' I said. 'I think it's dying.'

'Take her to the dam,' Holly said, because she thinks

I'm some kind of PA, put on the planet to look after her. I took the dog to the dam, watched it lap up the slimy water and when I came back everyone had gone. You get used to that when you're a teacher's son, your friends disappearing to smoke fags or sniff glue and aerosol canisters without you.

It had been an hour before I thought of something to say to Sarah and even then I didn't say anything. She blew a great big bubble; I saw it growing from the corner of my eye where I was sitting next to her on the grass. I put my finger straight up to her face and burst it. For a second everything smelt like fresh apples. That's what made me want to kiss her. I just pinned her to the ground and kissed her, my eyes wide open, her tiny blue eyes smiling up at me. Inside her mouth the chewing gum tasted more like cider. I found her tits under a thick vest but there was no shape to them. Her whole chest was like an old continental quilt, all soft and lumpy under its duvet cover. I kept on kissing her, my front teeth bashing against hers. She didn't flex a muscle, just lay there looking amused by me. When I had her bush in my hand, her pubes rough and scratchy, that's when I noticed the dog looking at me funny, its brown eyes staring down its long snout. I tidied Sarah's clothes up the best I could and ran away sniffing my fingers and I thought that was the end of it.

On Saturday morning – the next day – Kristian, Rhys Davies and me, we were sitting on the pavement in the street flipping two and five pence coins. It's the main thoroughfare, see, for the town. When it's sunny we just sit there watching women going shopping in cotton dresses, pushing prams with big, bald babies inside. Our street was built during the coal boom, my father said, a terrace with a row of small houses for the miners and their families on our side, and a row of bigger ones with front gardens opposite for the mine managers and supervisors. Johnny Mental was sitting on his porch wearing sunglasses, drinking lager, his teeth orange and ugly. Someone was painting their front door a few yards away, with a portable radio playing soul music: Diana Ross or some shit. A big burgundy Vauxhall Cavalier came around the corner, real slow like an old man on a hill, until it stopped next to us and I saw Jaime in the back looking worried, her eyes tiny and sinking back into her head. Her father got out, a tall broad man who looked like Tom Baker in Doctor Who, and he picked Kristian up by the collar of his best Kangol T-shirt because that's who he was closest to.

'You raped my daughter, you little prick,' he said. My stomach did a somersault inside me and got all twisted up. I looked at Jaime through the smoked glass of the car but she had the back of her head to me, looking at Johnny Mental. He'd stood up and was watching us; the lager can tilted in mid air towards his chin. Jaime's father punched Kristian in the midriff, cleverly so that none of us could see it, but we all knew it. 'Look at you – you dirty fuckin' paedophile,' he said to Rhys Davies John Davies and he spat on the pavement next to his feet. 'Won't be long until you're eating breakfast with your father, will it?' he said, but he didn't touch him. He picked me up by my ears, *by my ears*. My heart stopped beating then and my blood drained away. I don't know where it went but I felt it go.

'Was it you?' he said, and he knocked the back of my head against the brick wall of the house. 'Did you rape my daughter, you sick little cunt?' I could feel myself disappearing in his grasp when I heard Jaime shouting, 'C'mon. C'mon Dad, get in the car.' I heard the door slam behind him but it didn't sound anything like relief.

'You've gone all fuckin' white,' Rhys said, looking down at me when the burgundy car had been out of the street for a good two minutes.

'So have you,' I said, even though I couldn't see him properly. All I could really see was the bright yellow light of the sun but I imagined Johnny Mental smirking at me from across the road. I was thinking that if a stick in a bag was actually armed robbery then just having a cock could make a kiss and a crap fumble into a rape. I tried to look as confused as Kristian and Rhys were, as we all looked at each other, pale skinned and speechless, and I tried to drift back to myself.

I never really got there. My parents went to the town hall that night to watch a play about an old writer dying of the consumption. I went walking. I walked through the comprehensive school, even though I thought I'd done that for the last time after my exams three months ago. I didn't have the energy to lift my feet but at the same time they seemed to lift all by themselves. Over the running track I kept thinking about Sarah. I tried not to. I tried to think about words but the only ones which came were the ones that came out of Tom Baker's mouth with a spray of bitter saliva: *sick* and *paedophile* and *rape*. And underneath them I could see Sarah on the grass, smiling at me, her skirt hitched up her fat legs. There was no way it was rape or even molestation, she was fucking smiling at me, and she's fourteen, not a child. I'm not a paedophile. Jaime's sixteen and she's sucked the whole village's dick – that's what I told myself. But the longer I looked at the picture the more her smile turned into a frown, like looking at the Mona Lisa for too long, and she was starting to shake, her arms flailing on the ends of her wrists. Then I was here, on the railway track, lying down, the rails cutting into my hamstrings and the small of my back. I wasn't sure if I wanted to die. No, I didn't want to die. Not forever anyway, only until it was over, until it was all forgotten. I remembered Geography classes in school, where the teacher would talk about physics instead because he was a physics teacher really and we'd get bored and stare down here to the track and talk about how many people had died here. Kristian said there was a woman who tied herself in a black bag and rolled onto the track so that when the train came she wouldn't be able to get up and run. I didn't need to do that. I stayed perfectly still. Didn't even slap the gnats biting my face. When the train came, the clackety-clack rhythm it made froze me to the spot. I just closed my eyes. When I opened them again the train had gone, gone right past me on the opposite track and splashed my legs with black oil. I don't know now if I'm brave or just stupid. It isn't easy to be sixteen, see, and it isn't that easy to die.

But Not Really

It was summer. (But not really.) The sun, like a hot, green tennis ball, lit the lint and dust skating on the air of the bedroom. Through the white stripes of the Venetian blind. But it was hiding behind a slate-grey cloud, teasing. Jacqueline sat at her dressing table running a cotton bud dipped in Vaseline along the outline of her mouth, gently at first. And then harder and harder, as though she was finding herself, or recreating herself, painting her own lips onto her face and not just moistening the ones her mother gave her. She was thirty-three now. Funny, because she still looked seventeen, her 28-inch waist standing lithe in her chocolate brown cat suit, the zipper on it a chrome ring that balanced between her firm tits. There are people alive who would die to look like this, she thought, but beauty is like money. It means nothing when you have it and everything when you don't.

Her father was late. That's what her father was, late, for everything except work. For her birth, for her school play, for her wedding, for this pub lunch, and when he'd turn up he'd say, 'Don't fret Miss Onassis,' as though she was still his brunette ballet-dancing little girl. Yeah, some modern American princess she'd turned into. This was south Wales, and when she tilted her head back she could see in the mirror the abysmal hole cocaine abuse had burned through the septum of her pretty nose. The bedside phone rang. She ignored it. She didn't even look at it. She ignored, no, she shut out the sound and shut out the pungent ghosts she could see writhing on the filthy mattress of the walnut-frame bed: her bed. Instead, she fingered the brown envelope of her *decree nisi*. She was divorced now. It was over now. Today was the first day of the rest of her sweet life. (But not really.) Everyone knows you have to wait for the absolute.

Over the mountain, the lumpy planes of fresh green ferns, the arms on their stems uncurling, slow worms crawling underneath them, a twenty minute drive away, Graeme lay on his smoke colour draylon settee, the telephone cradle balancing on his naked waist, the receiver stuck to his face. A thin pink ring around his thighs where the white cotton of his underwear ended, before the orange self tan began. He stared around the baleful room, at the thick, drawn curtains. Through the wave of the cotton he saw Saturday morning light but he didn't know whether it was yellow or blue, or white or grey, and he would not stand up to check. Last night's cider bottles and beer cans were scrunched up into a sculpture of debris in the middle of his glass coffee table, lipstick-smudged glasses and a rotting odour. Around the edges, sticky tea and coffee circles from last week, or last month. He looked at the television, at the group of teenagers there miming badly, but dancing exceptionally well in small, bright clothes. He looked at the chair, and at Gemma sitting in it, her red pyjama top buttoned only at the waist to reveal her fifteen year old pancake breasts and her ribs rising like stairs to meet them, her face solemn between the pages of a magazine, his semen in her hair, turning it to thick strands of yellow straw. And the phone kept ringing. He tried to listen beyond it, to hear the sound of his house over the mountain, but he heard nothing. Probably, that's what made him angry.

'Bitch,' he said, and he gave up, threw the telephone to the old, stained carpet.

'I think he doth protest too much,' Gemma whispered, perhaps to Graeme, but perhaps only to herself, holding a page in the air, its numbers hidden on both sides under her thumb and forefinger.

'What the fuck's that supposed to mean?' he said, startled, looking at her ridiculous young body and her fatty, insolent face.

She shrugged her shoulders.

Graeme reached over and whipped the magazine from her lap but it was only a photograph of a blue-eyed, long-legged model, a leopard print slip and a baby tiger on a dog leash, the airbrushed gloss fake people hide beneath.

'I'm doing Shakespeare at school,' she said then.

'I know its Shakespeare,' he said. 'I know what it means too.'

'Well look at you,' she said, standing up, her voice ascending into a whine. 'Jacky this, Jacqueline that. It's got nothing to do with the house. You're always watching those stupid videos. You're obsessed.' Her whine wound down to tears, her face purpling. She snapped her top shut and stood awkwardly before his body, sprawled the length of the settee, her arms stretched out at the sides as if to demonstrate the madness of the situation. She gulped. 'Don't know what you see in the ugly old cow anyway.'

Graeme sat up and punched her.

In an Abergorki restaurant, fifteen minutes away now, Jacky's father scooped a forkful of pink flesh from his trout, and then stabbed the silver prongs into an *al dente* floret of broccoli. The food disappeared suddenly, like a fly you couldn't catch, into his parted grey mouth. Jacky watched as he repeated this procedure, over and over, broccoli first, then a carrot, and from another china-white side dish, a new potato swathed in golden spread. He didn't look up at all, just kept on eating, like a pig from a trough, his fatted temples dancing as he chewed. 'Do they have to speak Welsh here?' he said at one point. 'What a fucking God-awful language.'

But he didn't check, and didn't care who it was using the mother tongue he never knew, never learned, the choky words sounding to Jacky like a song that drifted with the food smells around the room. He was a millionaire, Jacky's father. (But not really.) Oh, he had the money, somewhere, and everybody knew it, even before she did. Before she knew what an E-Type Jag was he'd driven her to comprehensive school in one. The teachers stared out of the staff room window because it was unusual, no, bizarre to see money here, in this valley where poverty surrounded you like a neck brace. But in his own mind he was a poor man because he made the bulk of it after his thirty-fifth birthday. Apparently it wasn't worth as much then. He'd set a deadline for himself and he'd missed it. Since then he'd been working twenty-four seven trying to rebuild that burnt bridge behind him, the old fucking for virginity routine. Jacky tried to imagine him as a child with a red mouth, her grandmother spooning ice cream into it, saying, 'Open up, here comes the aeroplane.' But she couldn't. She couldn't ever imagine her father not being in charge. In her vision, *she* turned into her grandmother; lactation stains on the bust of her polka dot dress, and her father someone who wasn't conceived yet.

She jumped suddenly when his heavy knife squawked on his empty plate.

'What's the matter?' he said, brash, as though nothing could ever matter.

'Nothing Dad,' she said, lowering her head to him, ever conscious of the embarrassing pit behind her face, worried that he'd notice, although she knew he never would.

'Well are you going to eat that?' he said, pointing *his* nose at the cottage cheese salad curdling on her plate.

Jacky shook her head, pushing the food away from her.

Her father frowned, at the ceiling, not at her. 'Bad egg, Jack,' he said. 'Told you all those years ago. You wouldn't listen. He's gone now,' he said and he made a movement above the table with his fat fingers, a little boy running away with the snot still drying on his face. 'Don't fret Miss Onassis,' he said. 'You have the house, the money, your job, your freedom. You've won, baby,' he said smiling, knowing that him and his solicitor had won, and not knowing his daughter. 'Fuck him,' he said and he slapped a gold credit card on a saucer.

Later, Saturday afternoon, nothing but sport on TV – blue Lowry figures rolling around against a mud-red and grass-green background. Gemma prised the ring pull on a can of soda, Tsss. She held it firm to her mouth, the skin of her face tight, white paper under a thick, wet layer of sand colour concealer, already developing the silvery impact of a fist, her eyes pink like a soft albino animal's. In the silence of the empty room, past the light electrical snore of the mute television, she heard a bird sing outside, and further away, even lovelier, her friends at the back of Aberdare market, giggling, screaming, smoking spliffs in baseball caps and bra tops. She reached without moving her torso for a slice of notebook on the coffee table and caught it between her short, curling toes, struggled to read its text through the gloom on the wrong side of the closed curtains. *I've seen the film*, that's what it said, her script, her autocue, her line – to be delivered to her boyfriend's wife, down a telephone cable, on the hour, every hour. 'Try not to sound like a kid from Hirwaun,' Graeme had said. 'Try to sound like you're important.'

'I've seen the film,' she said, to the grey wall, her small voice insistent.

'I've seen the film.'

'I've seen the film.'

'I've seen the film.'

She picked the phone up and listened for a moment to the lonely clicking of the exchange. Then she put it down again. To a thirty year-old woman she was bound to sound like a school kid from Hirwaun; not any old kid though, she thought. Gemma was Tom Jones' daughter. (But not really.) Her mother had shagged him, that much was true. She'd heard her mother talking about it to the big fat Italian woman in the Bracci's; how they went to John and Maria's on Sardis Road every Sunday to meet, and how one day sitting on the bus to Pontypridd her transistor radio said that Kennedy was dead. But that was years before Gemma was born. Nobody knew who her father was, least of all her mother. Sometimes though, it was nice to think it could be Tom Jones, nice to think she was that close to an easy life, nice to think she could snap her fingers and be in a Los Angeles pool party away from this council estate, away from her illegitimacy; away from her bruises. Sometimes it was nice to think that she *could* be important. She picked the telephone up again then because she heard the front door latch go.

Greame stood at the porch smiling at her, the violet veins in his neck gone away.

'It's engaged,' Gemma said, her eyes frozen, the receiver limp in her hand.

He slid a pink velvet jewellery box out of his jean jacket. 'So are you,' he said.

That night, Jacky twisted in the pastel pink sheets of

her bed. Up and down the terrace pavements she heard the clicking of women's stilettos, half litres of vodka and white rum hidden in the secret pockets of their leather handbags, those few precious hours set aside for pure fun, Saturday night; alright for dancing, alright for drinking, alright for fighting. All Jacky had planned was sleep, but she couldn't do that, couldn't close her eyes and feel the hard ground, the cruel world slip away under her soles. The bedroom smelt bad, a bitter stench of sour breath, in the air, in the pillows, ghosts watching her, watching her furniture, breathing out sick and stale dioxide. However tight she screwed her face, her skin wrinkling like fruit, the evening light penetrated it, as though she had pin prick holes in her eyelids like the holes in the lining of her nose. Outside, hundreds of crows circled the town, swooping and shirking in graceful figures of eight: black spots against a magnolia sky. They screeched and squawked at one another in their fast, shrill bird language, warning something pivotal. Jacky was scared that if she fell asleep she'd never wake. Or even worse, she would. She turned onto her back and smoothed her hand into the cold sweat coating her hard, flat belly, looked at the ceiling rose, at its lips and curves, its shadow and light, the corners where dust gathered. She knew it like her own vagina. 'Fuck him,' her Dad had said. There was the problem; she'd already done too much of that.

Then the telephone rang and she answered it, fooled herself in a second that her father's imminent heart attack had arrived. Naked, cold, she held the receiver to her head and waited for the girl or for the man to spray their hot acid, the skin on her arms goosey. But it was Matt, the new boy at the estate agent, pissed, plucking up the courage to ask his blonde, rich, divorcee boss out for Sunday drinks, and she had nothing better to do. 'Yeah, see you tomorrow,' she said. Relief brought her sleep. But she dreamed of brown paper packages, all tied up with string. Videotape-shaped packages.

The next night, Sunday night, Gemma's bath night, Graeme drove over the mountain, his stomach heavy with his mother's doughy Yorkshire pudding. His tyres whipped on the black road as it curled and sloped unfathomably, like a stray pubic hair; sheep, their big yellow angular bodies squatting at the edge, the hot tar their campfire. Down in the next valley everything was dead. Everything except the Lucozade-orange street lamps. He drove, a thief in the night through the sleepy never-ending villages and blood-red stop signals until he got to the house, to his house. The moon shone against it, showing up its new paint, a soft lime colour, like a woman in a new layer of confidence, stepping out into the summer for the first time in a mini-skirt and a new pair of sandals. The hanging baskets either side of the front door, fuchsia trailing out: her grotesque earrings. He parked opposite and sat in the darkness, staring at its drawn curtains, its closed eyes. Inside, it was the same old No36. He imagined it, the chips in the banister, the scuffs in the bathroom tiles, next door's black cat crying at the kitchen window. Through a kink in the slat of the blind he saw the weak leg of the eight-seat dining table, and he thought he saw his wife dancing on it, kicking her lace knickers across the room.

(But not really.) His wife was in the street with another man, a younger man, laughing, her fingers smoothing the curled ends of her hair. He watched them fumble up to the door, this strange and ugly couple, the man's plump fingers making ripples in the loose polyester of Jacky's black dress. He wanted him to go in. (But not really.) To ravage her (but not really.) Graeme smoothed the palms of his hands along the thighs of his trousers, rubbed them until his skin was sore against the cotton, his heartbeat filling the car. When the boy turned out of the street, dawdling like a happy child around the corner, Graeme's muscles slackened, that's when the anguish came. He saw the light go on in the bedroom and he picked his mobile up from the dash.

'Hello?' Jacky said, her voice sugary.

'Jacqueline?' Graeme said, thwarting. 'You're still in my house. What's it going to take to get you out? Huh? We've had this chat before, remember? I get the house, or I get some compensation, or Daddy gets the tapes. Which part of this situation confuses you so much, baby? What's Daddy into, anyway? What would Daddy like to see Miss Onassis do? Anal? Would he like that? Girl on girl? Oh, I know, the gang bang. Hurry up now, Jack. I've got enough copies to cover your new boyfriend too. I'm sure he'd just love them, a youngster like that.' He pressed exit then: end of message.

Jacky curled up on the duvet cover, her arms clutching at her bony knees, her gold T-bar bracelet cutting into the mesh of her barely beige tights. *Revenge*, she'd thought when she'd put them on that afternoon, smoothing their wrinkles out along her calves. Greame loved stockings but hated tights. She laughed at herself out loud then, at her vulnerability, her stupidity. It had only taken her thirty-three years to discover there are just two types of people in this world: people who are wealthy and people who would like to be. No shit, Sherlock. Money makes the world go round! She tried to think about work, about selling houses, selling houses, selling houses, and she couldn't. She watched scenes from her life on the black ceiling, cine-camera footage of a chubby five year old, brown skin, brown hair, dancing naked on a Marbella beach, a school photograph of a miserable teenager in a fat knotted tie, she watched herself sway to a Carpenters' song, Graeme's hands planted on the backside of her taffeta wedding gown, her father's face in the background, his eyes livid, the champagne in his belly sharp like fish bones. Something changed then. The girl on the ceiling stopped smiling, stopped shining. She existed instead on flaky, amateur movies glaring hungrily out of the scene while strangers mounted her like an animal, a submissive blonde wreck with a twenty pound note rolled to her face.

It was easy at first: sex is the easiest thing in the world. Girls are preened for it from an early age; heels to make your legs look better, lipstick to make your mouth look as red as your cunt, taught to smile in the face of adversity. There's a woman faking an orgasm somewhere in Wales right now. But it got harder, it got dirtier, Graeme got nastier, all of it captured on celluloid. She was learning pretty quickly now; you cannot undo the love you once made. She thought of Graeme, forever whispering orders into her ears and suddenly remembered what the telephone was for. She picked it up and dialled out.

'What's the problem?' the woman said.

'Blackmail,' Jacky said. 'I'm being blackmailed.'

Outside she heard the church bell strike midnight.

That winter she sat in Cardiff Crown Court, the wooden bench hard against her arse, her black fur-lined full-length coat buttoned to the neck. Five years he got, not just for blackmail: for assault, and fraud, anything the powers that be could dig up. Jacky smiled meekly at her father sitting beside her and blew a huge sigh of relief. (But not really.) She already knew how it would work, saw the judge pick her father up for the Mason's meeting every Thursday for fifteen years, his veins full of single malt whiskey. Even the media stories fell in her favour.

Chickens

As a play-mate my grandfather was like a cheetah. His energy came in fast swoops but it rolled away again without warning and he'd need to rest again until his boring fatigue had passed over like a black cloud. He'd begun to wave his NHS walking stick in front of him, to detect pot-holes and kerbs, like a blind man, frowning perpetually, as though everything confused him. Ever since his knee joints had become inflamed, which seemed like forever ago, his stick had become a talisman, used once at Longleat Wildlife Park to gently push the roaming monkeys from peeling the rubbery windscreen seal from his gold car, only for the ringleader monkey to grab it and start hammering dents into his bonnet. The monkey seemed to smile in at us with his crinkled eyes, and laugh with a breathy cackle, like Mutley the dog, while I held onto my mother's hand so tight her fingernails began to bite into my skin, and everyone stared at the back of Tad's grey head, wondering why he didn't jump out and throttle it.

'Chelle bach,' he said, 'we'll need to go home soon. Mam-gu Blod will be looking for us.' He patted the flat top of my head, between my sprouting bunches and squinted at the goldfish he'd won aiming darts. 'And mind that fish now, don't drop him. Don't squeeze him too tight.'

'Just one more ride,' I said, looking through the murky water of the plastic bag at the red fish not swimming but floating inside. 'Just one more.' The fun-fair seemed to become more glamorous as the warm day turned into a cool and fuzzy evening.

Eventually my grandfather began to bribe me. He promised lashings of *Mr Creemy's* Neapolitan after roast dinner on Sunday; a return visit with two pounds spending money on Saturday and that evening, a glass of *Brains SA* beer he affectionately called 'whoosh', none of which interested me. But then he mentioned chickens. 'I'm going all the way to Glyn Neath tomorrow,' he said, 'because my chickens are getting old.'

'Why?' I said. I wasn't particularly asking why he was going to Glyn Neath or particularly asking why his chickens, like him, were getting old, but using the word as a prompt to prolong my time at the fair like the word *discuss* in an essay question keeps a student in his examination chair, his brain ticking.

'They don't lay eggs anymore, bach,' he said ignoring this question, 'and Mam-gu Blod needs eggs to bake sweetmeats for you kids. I'll have to get more. We need more chickens Chelle!' He stamped the grey rubber tip of his stick against the floor as though this confirmed his statement. 'If we go home for tea now you can come with me, all the way to Glyn Neath, tomorrow!' He struggled to smile through his pain.

I gritted my teeth and walked as slowly and as stubbornly as I could, without actually stopping. Getting to the fair in the first place had seemed like such a coup, it was a travesty, a tragedy, to leave. Every May holiday it stopped in our town for a week, the men with moustaches, rippling arms and tattoos sprawling over their naked chests dismantled and erected their vast metal contraptions on the wasteland in front of the rugby pitch, dog ends balancing in their lips. 'Jippo's', my grandmother called them, spitting, as though to shake off her own Romany ancestry. From her front window you could see the thin figures dance around the lot, transforming steel girders and cuts of canvas into rotating waltzers and ferris wheel cars. I'd patiently watch until the flashing neon lights were on, and then cry to go down. At this point Mam-gu would try to scare me, telling me that the men were thieves, and sometimes cannibals, and I gave up, frightened not by the travelling people but by my own grandmother's determination not to be in any way associated with them.

I was staying at my grandparent's house because my mother had gone away. 'Gone away', is all they said, which inevitably meant that there was more to it. In the six and three quarter years I'd been alive, she had never 'gone away'. I was clumsily shelling peas from their pods and dropping them into a ceramic bowl. I'd watched the dodgem track appear, and then the teapots, and then the red and white striped roof of the shooting gallery. My grandfather had merrily ventured into the living room while Mam-gu prepared gammon with pepper and butter in the scullery, singing *Calon Lân* loudly, warbling through the high notes, holding her hand flat on her big, left boob.

'Chelle bach,' Tad-cu said, seeing me stare out over the terraced roof-tops. 'Shall I take you down there? Shall I?' He put his finger to his lips, instructing me not to shriek. He took my small hand with his stiff, square fingers and happily, repeatedly shrugged his shoulders, like Tommy Cooper about to do a trick. I heard Mam-gu bellow as the front gate sprung closed behind us.

'Danny? DANNY?'

Danny was Tad-cu's real name. For a long time I'd thought the Irish song *Danny Boy* was written about him because he lived at the foot of a mountain side, and often, as though to deliberately exacerbate this, he'd cock his head and tell me he could hear the pipes calling. I ignored Mam-gu and struggled with Tad's inflamed knees down the hill towards the fair. At first he was delighted to be there.

'What do we want to go on first, bach?' he said, swinging his stick like a dance routine. We'd sat in a spangly red dodgem car and he'd steered it into a blue one a travelling boy was driving, the force throwing me into a mild shock and sending a series of blue and silver sparks across the circuit ceiling. I laughed wildly at his spectacles smoothing down his nose and his fine hair thrashing in the air. He eagerly reversed for good measure and rammed right into the boy's big shining backside again.

But now it was time to go. As we walked over the bridge, Tad, who needed support now from the handrail as well as his walking stick noticed the ducklings in the river below. Five brown baby ducks followed their brown mother duck in single file, like lemmings waddling along the pebbles at the edge of the water, the oncoming wind ruffling their soft feathers. They looked like little girls trying to walk in their mother's stiletto's, as I had done years before, but got smacked for scuffing the heels, or fell over and grew scabs on my elbows which my auntie checked daily to see I hadn't picked.

'Look Chelle!' he said, halting, 'ducklings. Have we got bread? What have we got?' Forgetting his sore bones, he knelt to the floor and fumbled with the bags in my hand, gently uncurling my digits, one by one, little by little to lift the candy floss out of my grasp, leaving only the fish. He scratched the cellophane open and broke cotton wool balls from the spun sugar. I frowned, hiding my eyes from the other children leaving the fair, my hands held like horse blinkers either side of my head. As a child, nothing can embarrass you as much as an adult to whom you are related.

'They're hungry, bach!' Tad said. He lifted me up over the railing so I could watch my clouds of floss blow like snow into the darkening river. The animal's beady, black eyes followed the pink flakes from the sky to the water but did not move from the river bank.

'They're not eating it,' I pleaded. 'Look Tad, it's just vanishing in the water.'

'That's their choice,' he said releasing me. 'The important thing is that we offered.'

I sulked all the way across the road, past the Red Cow pub and into Mam-gu Blod's parlour, my right thumb planted between my lips. Like her, I'd learned to roll my eyes at Tad's impromptu Dr Doolittle impressions but secretly I was impressed with Tad's ability to tolerate his own suffering when he thought he sensed suffering elsewhere, and I kept quiet, reminding myself to remember his strangely noble gesture.

My cousin Anna was sitting at the fold-out dining table in a velveteen pedal-pusher set, the colour of my absent candy floss, her cutlery set out before her and opposite, another place was set for me.

'Danny?' My grandmother roared like steam from behind the bead curtain in the scullery doorway. 'Where the hell have you been with that child?' She made *hell* sound like it had jumped from the mouth of a nun. A saucepan slammed on the draining board. 'I've been worried sick.'

'Never mind that, Blodwyn woman,' Tad said, taking the only bag we had left into the kitchen. 'Where's the salt? This goldfish has got white-spot.'

I sat down cautiously at the table looking at the crochet cloth instead of up at my cousin. I hated Anna, mostly for aesthetic reasons, her plaits were longer and lighter than my own, her dresses prettier. That weekend I hated her more than ever. The night before, I'd heard Mam-gu fretting through the bedroom wall. 'Oh Danny,' she'd said, 'what are we going to do? If she goes to prison?' her voice a low, unfamiliar hum. They talked about the details of the situation in Welsh and the most I could decipher was that my mother was on remand for stealing my estranged father's new car. 'We'll look after Michelle,' Tad had said, 'that's what we'll do.' I heard him drop his teeth into his tumbler of water. I didn't know what prison was exactly, only that robbers went there and I knew it was bad if it worried my grandmother. She had a nervous system like titanium. What was plain, is that it wasn't simply a case of going away, which had sounded nicer, albeit selfish. Now Anna reminded me of it all. She was there because she wanted to be. At night she'd go home again.

Mam-gu put our plates of ham, peas and salad down in front of us, her apron still tied round her waist, her tightly-permed grey hair flattened with sweat. She carried my grandfather's and her own meal through to the living room. I ate in silence, the pungent spring onions smell rising from the plate to tease tears from my eyeballs. After a while I noticed Anna was watching me carefully and slowly, mirroring my actions, even down to the foodstuff I chose to lift with my fork. She pushed her peas and shallots around in circles, her pink ham gone except for the soft, white rinds lying limp like dead snakes.

'Don't you like jibbons?' I said quietly, waiting for her taunt, or the punch line to her joke, knowing I'd be the butt of it.

'No,' she said dramatically, 'can't stand them.' She suavely popped a sweet pickle into her mouth. She was good at performing; she was going to be an actress. She was already Snow White at the Parc and Dare amateur theatre group. 'That's it,' she said, chewing it. 'I have finished.'

'You have to eat it,' I said.

'I don't, I'm going to throw it in the bin.' She shook her head so her gold braids danced.

'You can't,' I said, whispering.

'We can,' she said, 'watch.' Very slowly, as though the parlour was a safe in a bank, protected by laser alarms, she tip-toed to the bin in the corner and scraped her greens down into the rubbish with her fingertips. 'Now give me your plate.' I sat looking dumbly at her empty plate. Her hand gripped its edge, eclipsing the brown, floral pattern around the rim. It had to be some nasty prank in which she'd turn the blame on me.

'No,' I said.

'Do you want to have to eat all that?' She nodded at my mound of leaves as they turned purple with beetroot pickling juice. I passed my plate to her uncertainly. As she silently flicked stubborn lettuce from the plate I noticed my colouring book on the spare dining chair. Cleverly I ripped pages from its stapled centre and crumpled them into balls of yellowing paper, precisely placing them in the bin to obscure the awful food. According to my grandmother, oxygen was useless without a well-prepared meal to go with it, so getting caught disposing of fresh produce was not an option. She would have smothered me.

'Oh good, girls,' she said coming into the parlour and eyeing our progress, her tea tray loaded with crockery. As she passed, she stopped, as though able to sniff our nefariousness in the air and manoeuvred herself toward the bin. She stepped on its pedal, her enormous, round bum spreading oval as she bent to look inside. I held my breath as Anna's green eyes widened to the point of rolling out of their sockets. Immediately afterward, as though realising how silly an accusation it was, she stepped off the pedal and the lid crashed down. She shuffled into the scullery where I heard the oven door open. The hot, inviting aroma of strawberry jam tarts wafted out, choking the watery smell of salad.

Anna and I sat on the settee, Scruffy, our grandparent's three legged Yorkshire terrier separating us on the middle cushion like a pillow between reluctant lovers. Mam-gu was drinking Guinness from a pint glass. She was a feminist through and through, her fiery French mother's genes bubbling around inside her as she worked and scolded and cared, but if you had ever told her, she wouldn't have known what the word meant. Tad slept, blinking during his lucid moments at the recovering fish in its bowl on the table, or the television where Steve Davies was playing snooker. After bed time I heard my grandparents make an aggressive argument out of which cushion of the billiard table was the bottom, boasting a long and patience-sapping marriage with continuous ebbs of annoyance and easy flows of acceptance.

Tad-cu's garden stretched for an acre up along the uneven ledges of Maerdy Mountain. The stray cats scattered from their tinned stewed steak breakfasts left in rows on the clear, corrugated scullery roof, their triangular ears sent back on their heads by cautious irritation as I climbed the steps in my yellow wellies. Dew glistened on the grass blades. I hiked to the top of the garden, pulling on fern stems for support, avoiding the pet cemetery hidden behind a holly bush, which on less eventful mornings was my castle. Tad was in the chicken run, two small, freckled eggs caked in muck and ginger feathers balancing in his open palm.

'Tad,' I shouted, 'we have to get new chickens, remember!'

'After breakfast, bach,' he said clipping the gate behind him as the army of birds hopped towards us, jutting their funny heads quizzically. I didn't like chickens very much. What I was really looking forward to was a long journey. I loved being in transit because that somehow meant that life was on pause, and that was quite exhilarating. He gave me an egg to hold and we steadied one another back to the house.

'Are we going to eat those chickens when we get new ones?' I said.

He didn't answer me but scoffed as though it was a ridiculous suggestion. This after all was a man who trapped rats only to carry them in their cages to the top of the mountain and release them unscathed. He ate chicken, but never one of his own. They all died of old age.

'Know what I'm going to do?' he said. 'When you marry a prince I'll dig this whole garden over and find enough Welsh gold for your wedding ring! C'mon, let's give these eggs to Mam.'

In Glyn Neath, the egg factory sat unremarkable like a massive brown crate at the back of an industrial estate, the paint chipped from its zinc walls.

'Now hold my hand Chelle,' Tad said in a squeaky

wheeze, his nostrils tightened to black slits. Inside there was only the sound of machinery although hens lined the walls in box cages, balancing on one another in stacks, like Barbie dolls in Toys R Us. Florescent lights gave the warehouse a blunt and unnatural appearance. Tad talked with his new, high voice to a boy in an overall while I stared at the birds. They hadn't enough room to stretch their wings, let alone fly, and reminded me of the Return to Oz wicked witch's hundred heads, dead and locked in a cabinet, each one individual and capable of living, if only given the freedom.

'Why aren't they squawking?' I said as Tad pulled me away.

'They're probably too tired, bach,' he said.

'What's that smell?'

'Fear. Fear and poo and death.'

We walked back to the gold car and the boy in the overall followed, a twill brown sack clutched in his fist which moved of its own accord like a bag of magic potatoes. He passed it to my grandfather.

'Fiver,' he said. 'Not much use for eggs, them, but there's a fair bit of meat there.'

'You'd be surprised what a chicken can do when it's given free range,' Tad said dryly, although many of his chickens never laid eggs. They were left to live as normal with the ones that did. He put the bag in the boot of the car and paid the boy. We sat in the car for a minute, listening to the soft creaking a hen makes when it uses its legs for the first time. Then Tad leaned over into the hatchback and whipped the brown sack out of the gathering of heedful chickens. As he did, one small hen which had still been inside fell out flaccidly, its fleshy mohican which should have been red, was white.

'Is it dead?' I said.

'Michelle,' Tad said, taking it in his hands like a baby, 'it's not dead but I'm going to have to kill it. I have to put it out of its misery or it'll die in pain by the time we get home.' As he spoke he deftly twisted the hen's neck between his thumb and forefinger as though giving it a massage, which he did sometimes on my grandmother's big, knotty shoulders. 'It's for his own good Chelle,' he said, looking at me mysteriously for a moment as though wondering if I still loved him. He reached past me to the glove box for a plastic bag and wrapped the chicken inside it. He always had plastic bags on him, for collecting dandelion leaves for the rabbits. 'We'll bury it in the garden.'

'Is it dead?' I said again.

He nodded and started the engine.

My grandfather drove slowly over the peak of the dusty mountain. He drove slowly anyway on account of the infamous accident. When I was just a new born he'd backed his green Mini over the edge of a cliff with Mam-gu beside him. Neither of them were hurt but Mam never forgave him for having lost her knitting. (She'd been making a white cardigan with pearls encrusted around the cuffs and it flew out of the window. The wool was an off cut from Ponty market and she never, ever matched its ivory colour.) After a jolt, Tad'd check in the mirror that the chickens were okay. I could see them through my wing mirror. They huddled stiffly like one body of balding,

36

pimply skin with ten legs. Their eyes seemed to be focused on me, whichever direction they looked.

We stopped at the top of the valley for petrol and Tad left me in the car while he paid for it. I'd been sitting in the passenger seat for two minutes when one of the hens moaned from deep down behind its dirty feathers. There was a moment of silence before another hen followed suit. Collectively their noise sounded like a mass complaint, voiced with a woman's yelp. Volume seemed to give them confidence and they parted, pecking one another, like death warming up. The smallest, pale and shaking chicken didn't move at all. It sat in the middle of the boot while the others began to prod and butt it, its orange pupils fixed on me. Sometimes, animals instinctively knew when one of its brood was ill. Before my father became estranged, there was a fish tank in the living room and if one angel fish inside it became diseased, the others would push it to the surface of the water, like aquatic undertakers. I reached for the chicken, lifting it easily, like a toy.

Swiftly, I wrung its neck, as my grandfather had done. He made it look easy. In actual fact it was easy but I could feel its warm muscles moving and its life jumped from it with a bustling start.

Then the other chickens noticed me. The largest came towards the seat, flapping its wings and bucking like a frightened she-cat. The others followed, cocking their heads one way then the other as though they saw me through their ears, which I couldn't see but I guessed were situated somewhere around their popping, wan heads. At first I covered my own head and waited for it to stop, but it didn't, the other chickens joined in, wailing and striking my hands with their sharp and brittle beaks. It was important not to cry, because that meant I'd never collect chickens again. There was only one other solution.

'What have you done?' Tad said, his eyes circling the car anxiously where dead birds and emaciated feathers lay like litter. He lifted his fingertips to his temples.

'It was for their own good Tad,' I said. 'They were howling. They were in pain.'

'MICHELLE,' he said, and he was about to continue shouting, like the chickens, attacking me with thunderous nonsense, but words did not come. He sat down in his seat, placing his stick beside him, breathing quickly; his energy seemed to spill out of his pores, as his face turned somnolent in seconds. I gazed at the dry, red mud on my sunflower yellow wellies. After a while his jaw dropped and he spoke. 'I suppose they won't be much use for eggs after all,' he said calmly and he started the engine again.

One day in the playground I overheard Anna tell her theatre friends that the judge had thrown the book at my mother, not for her crime but for her insolence. 'Cheeky cow', she'd called her, her own auntie. I was never really sure if she had been acting, or repeating what the family said when I was out of earshot, or both. A year passed while she served her sentence, or as I preferred to think of it, tanned herself on a beach in the south of France. My grandfather didn't go back to Glyn Neath for any more chickens. Gradually the ones that were left stopped laying altogether. On the Monday after my failed gesture of nobleness, I asked Mam-gu for jam tarts.

'Oh Chelle,' she said, as though remembering something, 'we can't have tarts, there's no eggs.'

'There aren't any eggs in jam tarts,' I said.

'But there is, bach,' Tad said, 'in the pastry.'

'Can't we buy some eggs?' I said.

'Tad spent all his money on those chickens, cariad.' Mam said.

We had similar conversations for months on end. There was no scrambled egg for breakfast, no pies to go with our chips and malt vinegar on a Saturday, no Quiche Lorraine for days out, no Yorkshire pudding with our dinners, no hard boiled eggs in our summer salads and no Christmas cake at Christmas. Even at Easter when all the children in my class took eggs to school for the teacher to blow and then paint stripy with primary colours, I wasn't allowed to participate. It was amazing how much of life's foundation was made from egg. All along I had admired the way Tad had punished me. I realised how we needed to appreciate the things that provided for us, even down to the lowly battery hen, but I never thought he'd keep it going for so long.

At May when the fair was due again, an odd woman walked up our front path.

'Chelle, baby,' she said, 'come to Mammy.'

'My Mammy has got blonde hair,' I said backing away. Janet Goodwin, who lived in Anna's street, had escaped from a kidnapper the week previous and we'd had talks at school about not bothering with strangers.

She pulled me to her chest and smelt my scalp.

'I used to have blonde hair,' she said. Tears were

welling on her bottom eyelids and I could hear them too, in her words. 'God I've missed you. What do you want?' she said. 'You can have anything; let me get you a treat, anything in the world, a doll? A knickerbockerglory from Ted's Supper Bar? Say, what do you want?'

I wanted to push her away. *'Welsh gold for my wedding ring,'* I was going to say. *'My Grandfather'll get it, I don't need you.'*

'Come on Chelle, baby, say,' she said, pulling me tighter so I was hugging her without really wanting to. 'What do you want?'

I looked at my brunette mother. 'An omelette please,' I said.

The Joneses

I'm walking home from double science with Lipsy on a Thursday afternoon, past the asphalt running track and the Remploy factory. The Remploy factory is where Down's syndrome people make plastic chairs. Lipsy cracks some crappy joke about me going there when school is finished in two years, laughing through his nose. I tell him his mother's a fat whore who sends photographs to Readers' Wives. 'You wish,' he says. He takes his tie off and starts winding it round his wrist. The sun in the sky beats on my shoulders.

When we get closer to the terraces I can smell baby shit and chip fat. Dai Grudge comes running up behind us, red faced from the wanking contest behind the netball barn.

'A, Alex,' he says kicking a kerbstone with the rubber bumper on his big, stupid, blue trainers. 'Would ewe stick yer dick in Jasmine Jones?' Jasmine Jones is a fat-calved, blonde-mopped, big-titted fourteen year old with unbearable body odour, quickly making her way through Treherbert RFC under-nineteens.

'Fuck yeah,' I say.

'Fuck, an' me,' he says.

When we turn into Gwendolyn Street she's there. Not Jasmine, definitely not Jasmine: a different sort of woman, standing on her doorstep, surveying the street behind her shades, her dark hair tied at the back of her neck, her long freckly legs sticking out of a denim skirt. Lissa. I turn the handle on our new Upvc door.

'See yer, 'omo,' Lipsy says and he carries on walking up the street with Dai Grudge, kicking his bag along the pavement.

Egg and potato waffle for tea, the ketchup bottle standing on its head on the kitchen table in our basement. Mammy hasn't fried the waffle long enough. It crumbles to mash before I get it to my mouth. When I do, it tastes of zinc: a frozen, cold processed food taste. Mammy walks by, a lime green washing basket full of worn towels clutched tight against her chest. 'Don't scrape yer shoes against the table,' she says. 'I 'aven't bloody paid fer it yet.'

Outside I can hear her talking to old woman Jones over the fence. We're all called Jones in this street. Keeping up with the Jones' isn't just a saying here. Only Lissa isn't called Jones. She's different, exotic, Italian, or something: Marconi or Mazelis, a name you don't see in a pack of Happy Family playing cards. 'Have ew seen it then Ber?' Mammy's saying. 'The damage? E's a bit 'andy I reckon, givin' miss bloody 'igh an' mighty 'er comeuppance.'

'I 'eard it,' Beryl says. 'Tears an' God knows what. We didn't wash our dirty laundry in the street when we were kids, mun.'

Guess who they're talking about? Lissa. Right! Giving her a good licking with their dried up valley tongues, like she cares, like we care. And I know she hasn't been arguing in public because I would have been there to see it.

I'm upstairs just in time to see the arsehole pull up, husband, boyfriend, whatever, my face pressed up against the new, thick net curtain on my bedroom window; another blue parcel from the catalogue, not yet paid for. He goes in the house, all swagger and parade, gel in his receding hair, pointing his car keys, activating some expensive alarm system, not fit to touch a freckle on her hand. And I start thinking about blood piping out of nostrils, black and congealed in ear holes, knife wounds and butcher hooks, hard boots in soft bellies and numchuck bruises on white skin. One day, I'll do it. Who'd miss him?

When I wake up at three in the morning I'm still folded up on the windowsill, my sketch pad on my lap and a black biro sketch of myself hanging from a rafter, a thick rope with a knot I learned in cadets. Over the road the curtains are closed but I can see the electronic blue of the television through the gap. It's Lissa, I know it's Lissa. The arsehole will sleep peacefully through anything, the sweat from the thick black hair in his armpits trickling all over the bed.

Then I remember my dream. It's the one where I'm in the street with my skateboard and Lissa comes round the corner with groceries. 'Hey,' I say and I take her bag from her hand, carry it into the house. She smiles at me but it's not a good smile. It's charitable, merciful, not ecstatic or excited. That's the end of the dream.

The only word in it is 'Hey'. I'm not even American.

Monday morning, maths, me 'n' Dai Grudge are skulking back to the terraces after registration, raindrops the size of peanuts hitting the ground then bouncing back up again, Dai in a Granddad shirt, no sweater, no coat, showing of his purple shag tags. 'Wait 'til ewe try iss stuff, man,' he's saying, trying to keep his half-made joint under the lip on the roof of a garage. 'Pure Afghan.' I spray a big A on the roll up door. That's A for Alex, not A for Afghan. When he passes me the spliff I take a toke and keep it down for sixty seconds, tastes like pure oxygen. It comes out in a dark grey plume, in a smile, the shape of my mouth.

'Iss fuckin' soaps, butt,' I say.

'Like fuck,' he says.

I put my paint can in my bag, laughing at him, his nipples visible in his see-through shirt. 'I'm off anyway.'

She's standing on her doorstep in a negligée and I wish I'd brought the dope with me.

'Can I talk to you for five?' I say and she stands aside so I can walk in the house and stare at the 32-inch TV. Kilroy's discussing truancy.

'Coffee?' she says.

'I don't drink coffee,' I say.

'Tea?' she says.

'No.'

'Sit down then, I want coffee.' She goes into the kitchen and I watch the back of her legs as she does. I can hear her pottering around and I peer ferociously round the living room, but I don't know what I'm looking for. I peel a sliver of skin away from next to my thumbnail. Then I have to say something before I shake and run out of the front door.

'How come you're still in your nightie?' I shout.

'Because I've got nothing to dress for,' she shouts.

When she comes back she's got her coffee in a black mug with the word BITCH printed on it in gold calligraphy. She sits down on the settee opposite and looks at me, waiting for me to speak. In my head I see the scene from that film with Catherine Zeta Jones' husband, where the chick crosses and uncrosses her legs. I don't know why I'm thinking of that now. I look at a fish tank with no fish in it. 'So, er, this prick you live with, he your husband or what?' I say.

'Oh Alex,' she says. 'You know everyone in this street is called Jones. Why would I marry him and become a Jones too? Lissa Jones, could you imagine?'

'So he's not?'

'No.'

'Is he hitting you?'

'No. Why? Is the street getting a lynch mob together?'

'What's a lynch mob?' I say.

'Nothing,' she says, and she looks at the fish tank too, and laughs. 'Sure you don't want a drink? Pepsi or something?'

'No,' I say. 'I want to fucking be with you.'

'Be with me?' she says, standing up.

'Yeah,' I say, standing up.

'I'm twenty-nine, Alex.'

'Yeah.'

'You're sixteen, Alex.'

'Yeah.'

She's got coffee in her mouth and she wants to speak but she can't. I wait for her to swallow it and I hear the gulp. Then she smiles at me, that stupid smile I've seen somewhere before. 'How could you look after me? You're a school boy,' she says, and she's still smiling, playing with me.

'D'ya think that silly cow across the road'd be alive without me?' I shout. And then something else comes into my head. I know it's going to sound stupid but I have to say it because I want some respect for it, now. 'I'm the man of the house,' I say.

The smile goes and she folds her arms and holds them rigid across her waist. 'I'm sure you are, Alex,' she says, going to the front door. 'And it's sweet but I don't need you, I'm fine. I'm happy with Alan, honestly.' I follow her and she opens the door for me.

'That's his name is it, Alan?'

'Yeah, look, I'm flattered okay?' she says, her forehead wrinkling up.

'But I'm not trying to flatter you,' I say, walking down the steps. I don't look back, something my father taught me, don't look back. 'And I'm not very sweet,' I say, heading for the lane quickly, so my mother doesn't see me.

It's Tuesday when I go to the insurance office, wheeling down the gravel on my skateboard, good skateboard too since I put new wheels on and I haven't got cash for the bus, knife in my pocket, don't know what sort of knife, a kitchen knife but too sharp for vegetables, too blunt for meat. I see Lipsy in the High Street with his father but I skate right past, right down to the DS Howell's sign, illuminated orange in a window. I wait outside, edging my forefinger along the blade. At one point I nick myself but I won't take my finger out, look at it and miss him.

When he comes out he walks right past me.

'Oi,' I say.

'Orright butt,' he says turning to me, then he turns around again and makes to walk off.

'Alan Jones,' I say and he ignores me.

'Alan Jones,' I say again.

'What?' he says.

'Crap name i'n' i'? Jones?' I say. I'm looking straight at him and I can see a clump of black hairs coming out of his left nostril, and sweat patches under his arms.

'What's your name?' he says.

'Jones,' I say smiling.

An old woman shuffles past and gives my board a dirty look.

I take the knife out of my jacket and start cleaning dirt out of my fingernails with its tip. Alan's about to walk away again. 'But some Joneses are different to others,' I say. 'Like some Jones' are older than others. Some Joneses are cleverer than others. Some are nicer lookin'. Some Joneses like hittin' wimmin, and other Joneses don't. Know what I mean?'

'Not really,' he says. 'I've got more important things to do than stand yere listening to yer shit.'

'I know,' I say. 'You've got that lovely redhead to look after, now; her name isn't Jones, is it? She never wants to be a Jones does she? So you don't own her, do you? You never will, like. She's not your possession, is she?' I'm shouting.

'Whatever, kid,' he says taking a step back from me and my kitchen knife.

I point the edge of it between his onset of flabby tits, and I say, 'I'm watching you, Alan Jones!'

On Saturday night I'm coming home from football, first time I've been to soccer for a month, when I see them driving down Glanaman Road in his shitty, silver Sierra. Alan doesn't even see me. He's concentrating on his speedometer, fifteen mph. Lissa's got a strappy summer top on. I wink at her and she smiles all coy, peering over her sunglasses.

Five yards up the road I can see Lipsy in the kid's park trying to make himself dizzy, pushing the little roundabout round, as fast as he can until he lifts his feet off the ground and spins with it. Jasmine Jones is sitting on it, grass blades in her matted hair. I squeeze through the railings and sit on the floor next to Dai Grudge. He's got a plastic container in his hand, holding it to his face.

'Hard as nails Al,' he says, showing me the glue. 'Trippy as fuck.'

'It's wallpaper adhesive,' I say. 'It's not gonna ge' you 'igh, like.'

'Well I'm skint in I?' he says.

'Giss yer nip on tha' then Jazz,' I shout as she lights a menthol fag.

'Iss my last one,' she says.

I whip a fiver from my jeans; here's one I stole earlier. 'Well come for a walk with me,' I say, 'and I'll buy you some more.'

She jumps off the roundabout going arse over tit. I get up and walk over to pick her up, closing my nostrils and breathing through my mouth.

The Magician

The cars snaked along the motorway, following one another in and out of the fast lane, their oblong, metallic rooves synchronised in direction and time, like the carriages of a child's pull-along train. The sky above them was grey and uncertain. It was spring bank holiday. Naomi's horoscope had told her that she was a strong, if somewhat impulsive person, capable of dealing with May's disasters, but she didn't contemplate disaster. Horoscopes were like that; hazy and improbable. They were never concise. She wanted concrete truths. She wanted to know if what she wanted to happen would happen, and how, and when: the details, the dates, right down to the hour so she knew when to apply her lip gloss and best scent. They never told her anything, anything she wanted to hear at least, but they were her only window. She couldn't ask anyone else's opinion so she kept trawling through the pages of tabloid supplements, desperate for sweeteners.

'You want yours?' she said, looking up from the magazine at Ed next to her, his eyes on the road.

'Aye, go on,' he said. He claimed not to believe that the alignment of planets or stars could tell him what would happen in his life, he didn't believe in God or in ghosts or even in intuition. He didn't believe in anything which wasn't glaringly obvious but he would do just about anything to indulge Naomi.

'Pisces,' she said, her voice becoming supercilious as it did when she read aloud. 'You'll need to take the bull by the horns this weekend as you become aware of somebody leading you up the proverbial garden path. Issue ultimatums and stand firm.'

'What a load of shit,' Ed said.

Rain began to spot lightly on the windscreen. Naomi closed the magazine, slugging from her warm bottle of lager. She turned to the window, focusing her attention on the road, and a squashed hedgehog in the middle of it.

Near Taunton, Steve aimed the lit end of his joint out of the gap in the BMW window so that the ash flew off in the wind, but the amber point went with it, leaving a shallow hollow in the paper tube. 'Oh fuck it,' he said, his voice quavering, heavy with intoxication as it had been since anyone could remember. He threw the thin, half smoked spliff on the dashboard.

Katie regarded him for a moment. He was frowning intensely through the windscreen, his eyebrows scrunched into a fat pucker. The fake tanning lotion he insisted she smoothed onto his face the previous evening streaked in orange clouds around his blonde hairline and animate brows. The whites of his eyes were yellow with cirrhosis. He looked like a big jaundiced baby. She turned back to the road, both saddened and amused by his appearance. Alcoholism, like Alzheimer's, was a disease you had to laugh at, before it made you cry. Nobody ever mentioned that Steve was dependent on drink, although they all knew it, every one of them. He was expected to look stupid.

'When are we stopping for a piss then?' he said. 'Dyin' I am, mun.' He'd said this twice since they'd begun their journey in Wales, three hours ago, and each time Katie had said nothing, nodding her head to the dull guitar song on the radio, hoping he'd forget his request, as he quite often did.

'We're almost there,' she said.

'Dyin' I am Kate. I'll 'af to go over your nice seat otherwise.'

Katie flashed her lights at Ed and Naomi in the blue Renault Clio in front of her, and they indicated into the nearest lay-by. The third car, oblivious to Ed's attempts to capture their attention had driven on ahead.

Naomi watched Steve urinate against a thorn bush through her wing mirror, on the unimaginative stretch of the east Devon motorway, while Ed studied his tyres, prodding them without any real intention. The liquid ran backwards past Steve's grubby, white trainers, hot against the grey concrete. Naomi would have liked a piss too, but that meant peeling her jeans down her thighs and baring her white arse to the world. If she'd worn a skirt, she thought, if she'd worn a skirt.... But she never did reach a conclusion on how much easier women's lives would be if they wore skirts like men thought they were supposed to, because Jack had appeared in the lay-by, walking towards them, his pallid face curious.

'There's Jack!' she said, forgetting herself. Their eyes rested on one another for the briefest moment, just enough for her to reregister his squashed, livery Cupid's bow mouth. Then the others congregated around him, whooping beside her open window.

'Fancy seeing yew 'ere!' Jack said, watching Steve as he clumsily zipped his fly. It was something he said often, to extenuate his comical Cornish accent, although it had never seemed so appropriate.

'Yeah, how come?' Ed said, suspiciously.

'I told Charlie I'd meet you here, the last lay-by before the junction for Exeter. Where is Charlie?' He made to glance into the Clio, as though Charlie was in there, but he knew he wasn't so he averted his eyes, back to Ed.

'Gone man,' Steve said. 'We only stopped for a piss.'

'Well what a fucking coincidence,' Jack said.

'Yeah, what a coincidence,' Jo said, slamming the passenger door of Jack's Celica. She joined them in the queue for Charlie's inevitable return, her red, wavy hair whirling in the wind behind her and landing on the narrow shoulders of her fitted brown leather coat.

What a coincidence. Naomi became aware of her hooded sweater pulled down around her shoulders for comfort, and her naked feet, propped on the seat before her. The sun was there, amid a cloud in the west of the sky, but she had goose pimples along her blonde-haired arms. She pulled her fleece top up and around herself and gripped her fingers tightly around her empty green bottle, lest anyone notice that they were shaking. And she froze, until Lyn and Charlie's blood red Volvo came bombing and beeping up the other side of the motorway.

Jack walked with a bounce back to his car, quickly patting the wing on the passenger side of the Clio, which only Naomi seemed to notice. Everyone else was belting up. 'Remember you're in England now,' he called, as he bent and disappeared into his own car. As he did, she dissolved, her blood vessels cooing.

'He's right,' Ed said, though it hurt him to say it, nodding at the car in front of him after they'd driven another thirty miles along the A30 towards Bodmin.

'What?' Naomi said, waking from her daydream.

'Jack. He's right. We're in England now. We're going camping with a bunch of strangers. They're all dealers, Charlie said. Sales fodder, we are. They're gonna give us pure ecstasy so we come back, to buy it next time.' He squeezed Naomi's kneecap without taking his speckled green eyes from the windscreen, and the driver in front. He knew the length and breadth of her body, the pulpy texture and musky smell of her skin, every bone, scar, nick and cavity, and after four years sharing a bed with it, it still delighted him. 'Don't take anything that's not Welsh,' he said, 'and watch your drinks.'

Naomi nodded. She unclipped the butterfly grip at the back of her head and fingered her loose, thick, dirty blonde hair. But they were not in England, she concluded. They were in Cornwall, where her great-great grandparents had come from when they arrived in the Welsh valleys to mine coal, and seeing as she hated Wales so much she thought some part of her must still be left here. She wanted to look for it in the harbours of fishing villages, in the surf, in the tin, in the watercolours of St Ives, even in a rave on Bodmin moor. As a child on holiday she'd sat with her father on a bench in Falmouth town, as an old lady with a tartan shopping trolley had approached. 'Don't move too fast,' the woman had said, 'but there's something behind you.' When Naomi turned in her seat she saw a red squirrel for the first and last time, a chunk of chocolate prised in its tiny, human-like fist, its pleasured, chewing face unperturbed by the traffic sailing passed. She'd thought that the lady was a white witch who'd made the rodent appear, simply to entertain her, and that everyone in Cornwall was capable of sorcery.

The moor opened up in front of them, bare and desolate, and dotted with sheep yet to be sheared. The cars lined next to one another on the spitting gravel, so Naomi's window was adjacent to Jack's, but she only looked forward, at a wild pony standing at a distance on the top of a blue grassed tump.

'Okay, let's get the tents,' Ed said, and car doors opened and popped shut around them.

At the party that night, the small field surrounding the host's farmhouse was full. The band played Jimi Hendrix songs but the eighteen year old girl singer wasn't experienced or desperate enough to convey the words in any meaningful way. Her low voice bubbled out from behind her curtain hair, totally obscured by the bass drum and guitar licks. Katie, who was a hair stylist in a salon named after its own postcode was sitting on a haystack, smoking pot, her eyebrows plucked and raked into a cruel angle. When she lifted the humorously-lengthed joint to her lips, her false fingernails hid her neat chin. Lyn next to her, as though constantly aware of Kate's profession, smoothed her drying, bleached curls onto the opposite side of her neck. The lights from the house caught the diamantes on their clothes and the dusty eye shadow above their eyelids. Charlie was dancing alone amidst a throng of greying farmers who all had bottlenecks of French red wine tilted to their mouths. Every half hour or so he'd produce a creased baggie from his fleece jacket and stab his middle fingertip into its powdery contents, sucking it quickly and crumpling the bag away again for future reference. Naomi stood between Ed and Steve. Steve widened his eyes frequently so that Ed could see the pink veins leading away from his pupils like roads on a map leading away from London. 'Good iss, ini?' He said each time, and opened another foaming can. Jo was standing in front of the open French doors, on the crazy paved patio with a group of women, unknown to Naomi, two of whom were heavily pregnant. Now and again, threads of their conversation floated over to her on the breeze and it seemed to concern old school dinners and gym lessons with suspected lesbian trainers. Occasionally Jo and Naomi's eyes met over the crowd and they smiled politely at one another, only to draw away again. Jo struck Naomi as slightly quirky and complicated, her red hair and red lipstick never matched and she only had one going-out halter-top and one pair of black stiletto heels. She always appeared uncomfortable, as though wherever she was, she'd prefer to be somewhere else, inviting sympathy rather than jealousy. At first, Naomi had guiltily avoided her and when this became impossible she'd over-compensated, finding herself taking a chair to her when she was standing, or complimenting her unattractive jewellery. During this stage of their acquaintance they'd confided in one another that Katie was a bad hairdresser and discovered they'd both thanked and tipped her for new colour, only to cry in their car mirrors on leaving. That stage was over and they seemed to be moving into a new quiet phase which only featured practical questions, like 'do you know where Jack is?' or, 'do you take sugar in your coffee?' Naomi spied around. At one point she'd spotted Jack behind her amidst a hushed yet physically dramatic discussion with a skinhead whose facial zits were about to burst. Jack's black shoulder-length hair which was usually sticky shone under the Chinese lantern. His hand was planted into the arse pocket of his jeans. She looked at both his arse and his thin, fawn wrist growing out of its pocket for what seemed like a very long time. But now he was nowhere. It was a bit past midnight and she decided to go back to the campsite.

She woke in the night to the sound of an English woman's pungent laughter, echoing from the distant farmhouse. Dance music was still pumping but the human voice pierced through it. She knew instantly that the woman was English because the Welsh were not capable of such chutzpah, not in a country which wasn't their own at least. Her torso was constricted by Ed's hard, builder's arms, his tight hands pinching the skin around her ribs despite her layers of clothing. Her bladder was expanding in her thorax and it was cold. It was icy cold. Ed had bought the biggest, best tent in the department shop and it had taken seven of them to erect it while she laid Ed's denim jacket over the daisies and sat down with another beer. Jack, who was threading a pole through the seam in the dome roof had said, 'I'm building your home here, and you're not doing *anything*.' She'd simply nodded, too sober to bother thinking up a flirty retort. Outside, all of the domes were covered in a film of thin frost. One outdoor candle still flickered against the cobalt sky. In the tent opposite she heard rustling and she stood still on the grass to listen.

'C'mon, cwtch up,' she heard Jo whisper. Instantly she felt a stem of contempt rise up into her throat. Surely it should have been Naomi who used that expression, not Jo, who was not Welsh and who had already shared a bed with him for close to a decade. She squatted behind her own green tent and urinated between her nylon socked feet. As she did she noticed a coffee coloured pony watching her quizzically from behind the nebulous foliage and considered chasing and riding it. It would canter her away from her claustrophobic circle of friends, the warm smell of its fur thick in her nostrils. She decided that she was still pissed and she stumbled back onto Ed's mattress, purposely, noisily clasping the velcro of the door together after herself.

By morning, the frost had melted. The sun burned through the canvas so that even the oxygen was hot. The farmhouse patio was littered with last night's debris. Bottles, mugs and cans carpeted the ground. A few people sat in a semi-circle on the dew-damp haystacks, a camp fire smouldering noxiously between their knees. One of them was Steve, his red eyes still wide, although the heat from the flames had stripped one side of his face of its tan. He gulped from a full bottle of wine he'd discovered breathing beside the stage. Next to him, one of the farmer men dozed, cocaine rocks caked around his running nose. On the floor the outline of two bodies showed through a scratchy cerise blanket, only the soles of their black trainers visible. Acid jazz blared from the speakers but it seemed to drone now rather than encourage.

In the bathroom, Ed held Naomi's hand, lightly clutching at her fingertips while she heaved, her eyes and nostrils closed to the dank stink of the lime-scale stained pan underneath her and the cardboard toilet-roll carcass beside her. He only let go to break thick, white ruffles from the new roll he'd carried with him from the tent and hand them to her, bit by bit. He watched her rub herself roughly and quickly, embarrassed by his presence and glad that the experience was almost over. She was much younger than him and she expected romance and spontaneity in a relationship. Soon she would appreciate a man who'd wipe her arse for her, and the familiarity and security he brought with him. But for now life was fast and youth was wasted on her. 'I'll wait outside now Ed,' she said fastening her jeans.

She walked through the filthy kitchen, wiping her cold hands on her thighs. The boy with spots was eating toast at the table but she ignored him. On the patio, the few people awake were crowded around a body on the floor.

'Oh fuckin' hell! Are you Welsh?' somebody said as she approached. 'Are you with Jack? Do you know this fella?'

Steve was unconscious, his head wedged between the dry stone wall and a log, half covered with cracking bark. Blood projected in a black stream, spraying a line of graffiti onto the wall. Everyone stared, as though waiting for the one decipherable word.

'Bad that,' the farmer said. 'Heard his skull crack there. Nasty that. Should 'ave seen it. One minute he's fetchin' wood for the fire, next he's sliding down there. E's mad, im.'

'I'll have to ring an ambulance,' Naomi said.

'Yeah, careful though love,' someone said, 'cos he just took some pills. Orange they were, didn't say what they were, looked serious they did. Wouldn't give me none neither.'

'What shall I do then?' she said, panic setting in. She was a wallflower in a crisis.

'Phone an ambulance,' Ed said, calmly pushing into the spectators with two grubby, blue tea towels balancing on his forearm. 'You'll have to Nai, it looks bad.'

'Use my phone,' the skinhead said, jittering in the doorway. He held his tiny handset at arm's length.

When an ambulance from Truro hospital arrived twenty-five minutes later, Steve was awake but his vision was blurred. He was laughing at an inaudible joke, told by an apparition in a rain cloud, his head resting on Ed's blood-soaked lap. Everyone else sat in grave silence while the paramedic parted Steve's hair and wrote things down. After a while she walked him to the vehicle and Ed followed, blowing Naomi a fat air kiss. 'I'll be back soon,' he said, 'the car keys are in the cooler bag.' His voice trailed away so she only saw him mouth the words, 'I love you.'

That afternoon, after some loud but ultimately lazy campsite hysteria over Steve's accident, Naomi and her friends were sitting around a pub lunch in the nearest village. There was only one stainless steel gravy boat to share between six of them, which had angered Lyn immensely.

'I like gravy,' she said. 'I like gravy a lot.'

'But in England we only put gravy on our meat,' Jo said. It was hard to tell if she was being sarcastic or not. A parrot in a cage beside the bench squawked obtrusively, ending the strand of conversation. Everyone turned to look disconcertedly at the creature as it began to pluck its feathers out with its curling beak, making larger the bald patches beneath its enormous wings. Katie, who'd dropped two grams of amphetamine, and who had been wondering what to say next, said, 'Mad tha' parrot ini? I've never seen anything like tha' before.' She took a deep breath which whistled ominously between the gap in her front teeth. 'While we're here as well, I jus' wanna thank Jo and Jack for inviting us to where they're from, 'cause it makes a nice change from home, even though Steve has smashed his skull in, and there's not enough gravy to go round. Serious now, thanks Jack.'

'Steve is going to be okay,' Jack said. He'd said this many times at the campsite, like a mantra to convince himself as well as Katie.

'Yeah, Kate,' Lyn said. 'Steve is going to be okay. Probably by the time we get back Steve and Ed will be there.'

On mention of Ed, everyone turned to Naomi, so Naomi used their attention to speak. 'This is the Jamaica Inn isn't it?' she said suddenly and adamantly, rolling her head around the room. 'Daphne Du Maurier wrote a book about it, didn't she? "Alone in glory, four square to the winds," she said.'

'Yeah!' Jo said.

'How do you know that?' Jack said.

'Because I'm a bit Cornish,' she said, looking straight into his eyes. She'd told him this before but he seemed to instantly forget anything she said. He was a habitual pot smoker with acute short-term memory loss.

'Oh yeah, you said that before,' Jo said, and her interest in Naomi slipped away as the others had, as soon as she'd mentioned a foreign name and a book. All her friends were excited by was the prospect of getting shit-faced after a long week of work. Nobody had time for a novel but she tried to accept this because Ed had told her once that everyone was cultured in their own way, and she'd wanted to believe him. But Naomi felt Jack's eyes lean on her for another minute while she elegantly stabbed and devoured her butter-soaked julienne carrots. She felt homely in a Cornish pub fogged with myth and legend, and tried to imagine sitting at the same table in the eighteenth century, in a cold winter, waiting for the men to return, wet and windswept with their contraband hidden in hollowed tortoise shells. She was alone in the Smugglers' Museum adjoined to the bar when he crept up to her, coiling his arm around her waist. She saw his dark hair reflected in the cabinet door, but his eyes were muddy. She jolted against him, keeping her own eyes on the wax-work pirate in the case in front of her, pretending to be more interested in it than in Jack. 'Nai,' he whispered knowingly. 'I'm sorry. I couldn't get away last night. I was arranging something. Listen to me now. I'm going to offer pills around when we get back to the tents. Don't take one. Say you're waiting for Ed to come back. They'll think they're E, but they're not. You mustn't take one, or even share anyone's. Got me?'

'What are they then?' she said.

'Sleeping tablets. They're all going to sleep,' he tossed his head towards the bar dismissively, 'but *we're* not.' His hand smoothed her hip, his fingers pressing, eager and hungry. 'They're waiting in the cars anyway. I said I'd get you. Go back with Kate and I'll see you later.'

She yielded easily to his suggestion, nodding through the mirrory glass and turning to follow his jaunt out of the pub, her skin tingling. At the door, the barmaid waved farewell.

'Thanks guys,' she said smiling. 'And mind how you go – there's a beast out on them moors!'

Naomi giggled incredulously.

From the green, sloping field where they camped, Jack could see the lonely hillsides he'd grown up amongst, specked with the cloudy, yellow fuzz of sheep and the new white of springing lambs. To become an adolescent in such a barren area turned a boy into one of two things: a farmer or a rebel. And Jack was the latter. At fifteen he'd forged a little contraband business of his own and it had matured into something which was no longer little. Two years ago it had turned itself into a franchise, which meant he'd set up home in the Welsh valleys, which were flooded with murderous class A shit, but starved of party starters. He cheered it up, decorating it with biccies and amph and smoke, driving its main roads in his valeted Celica, like an ice-cream man selling vanilla wafers. But he wasn't ambitious. He was a drug dealer simply because he couldn't be arsed to do anything else. It was so easy, and what he liked most was the people it brought his way. Naomi had been flirting with him for eighteen months, and it had taken him this long to do something about it because Ed clung onto her constantly and Jo clung onto him, like jackdaws who'd found gold. If he got caught cheating he'd be stuck with Naomi, and hot women didn't cook or clean, they just expected new shit all the time, new clothes, new shoes, jewellery. He couldn't keep her forever. He'd rather Ed did that. When he wanted to put somebody to sleep though, he didn't fuck around with Nytol. The orange pills in his pocket were pure codeine.

'Come on then kids,' he said sitting up to toy them from his jeans, placing their chalky plastic container on the ground beside him. He tied his hair back into a rough ponytail which he did when he was nervous, or when he meant business. 'Grub's up.'

Naomi hadn't believed Jack when he said that he was going to drug everyone. She was just happy that he'd found the energy to follow her, deceiving Jo. He never phoned when he said he would, never made it to the pub when she was wearing her best dress, never made it to Ed's house when he threw a party. She submitted to the possibility that there would only ever be rushed gropes in dark nightclubs and quick, hard horse kicks under tables, and sometimes she reluctantly admitted that this was all she wanted anyway, a little taste of danger. She'd watched sceptically as her friends lined up for tablets, calmly sipping her ruby cabernet from its white paper cup, half believing that it *was* ecstasy Jack was issuing, that he was deliberately trying to exclude her. But she realised something strange was stirring when Charlie burnt himself with his own cigarette.

'What the fuck are you doing?' Lyn said, scolding him, but she was slurring. She tried to take the cigarette away from Charlie, to smoke it herself, but she gave up moving towards him and slumped back onto her scatter cushion.

'This is lovely, this,' she said, and she closed her eyes, her weight falling out around her.

Jo was the last to hold onto consciousness, although the bones in her body had disintegrated. She melted into her camping chair, her red hair falling into her face.

'Look at you,' Jack said, looking at her. 'You're 'angin', Christ, you're always hangin' Jo, but you really are, you're a mess,' and he laughed, turning to look at the grass between his feet. A spurt of dribble bubbled out of Jo's lips in defiance, but by the time it had dried on her chin, she was gone. Naomi felt a pang of disgust stab through her veins because she liked Jo more than that. She at least didn't think that she was hanging. In a second however, it was pushed aside by her heart beat, the heavy thrum which always appeared when Jack's eyes were on her.

'Let's go,' he said, rising victoriously and she walked with him to the other side of his Celica, her cup of wine squashing under the pressure of her clammy fingertips, and Ed's blue denim jacket dragging behind. When they sat, the knees of their crossed legs touched. It was bizarre to be able to sit as close to Jack as she liked, and look into his coal black pupils. His eyes were startling. When she began staring at him, she could never stop, because they looked like ebony holes where you could bury yourself. Once, over a pub table, they'd locked sight on one another and she hovered over him like a girl at a cliff edge, until she felt the falling sensation towards sleep and her belly against the table. She'd lunged back into reality and noticed that Kate had been watching her. It'd felt like hours. But Lyn was still at the bar ordering a round of Pernod. Only minutes had passed.

'You've got eyes like a blue bottle,' she said, and she drained her cup of its viscid contents. 'Do you know that?'

'My eyes?' he said. 'They're glassy because I had laser surgery five years ago. Before, I couldn't see a thing. Now,' he nodded at the ponies on the mountain, '20/20 vision.'

She sank away from Jack, leaning on the ground behind her, disappointed. His eyes *were* only holes, not a tunnel leading to paradise, but gouged and empty pits. She didn't know him. He tried to pull her towards him by the waistband of her jeans but she slapped his hand away. She'd always imagined that it would be impromptu, zealous, neck-biting, clit-flicking, that fate would buy them time and privacy.

'This isn't right Jack,' she said. 'We were supposed to get a hotel room or something. You can't just drug everyone. Do you think you're God? Do you think you're a fucking magician?'

What she wanted him to say, was yes. She wanted him to confirm his superiority, his power, his wit, but he only laughed sarcastically and said, 'Black magic. I think I can do black magic,' and she knew that he was only a man.

'It's sick, Jack,' she said.

'It was expensive,' he said, frowning.

Naomi put her head down on the grass, her hands pressed together as though in prayer, beside her face. She closed her eyes but the sun still shone purple through her lids. All she could hear was the light chatter of birds, and Jack's frustrated breathing above her. The morning's events had exhausted her nervous system. There was no adrenaline left.

She dreamt of Africa. She saw crazy medicine men administering anaesthetics, only to bury their patients when they did not wake, but at sunset they rose out of the sand, dusty, braying, like horror-movie zombies. As she watched, they turned into her friends, dark with naked, swinging breasts, their eyebrows shaped and with ash blonde ringlets. She saw Charlie slide along the beach like a Sidewinder, his legs backward and useless. She saw Jo stretch up on her knees, blood pulsing from her throat like vomit. She saw Steve lying in the white grit, his neck broken. And when she woke up screaming, it was green pupils she looked up into, not black.

Ed held her to his chest until she woke properly, her own chest pumping, her scalp sweating. 'What's going on?' he whispered. 'Everyone's asleep, what are you doing over here on your own?'

Naomi rubbed her eyes with her fists and peered about. Jack's blue tent had gone, as had his car, as had Jo and the camping seat she'd been sitting in. Ten yards away Lyn and Kate slept, spread eagle on the cooling ground. Charlie was snoring.

'Oh, too much wine,' she said and she reached for the empty paper cup, which was still there, as though it proved her drunkenness. 'Is Steve okay?'

Ed looked around the field, raising the ball of his nose to the air as though he smelt a lie in it, as plain as cooking wafting from the farmhouse. 'He'll be okay,' he said, 'but he's concussed, they're keeping him in. His blood was choc full of codeine.'

'What's codeine?'

'Opium, methadone. Smack, sort of.'

'What a wanker,' Naomi said, glancing at the patch of grass where his Celica had been.

'Who?' Ed said, summoning her eyes back to his face.

'That skinhead freak,' she said, blushing. 'It was him who gave him that, I'm sure it was.'

'Where's Jack?' Ed said.

'I don't know. He was here before.'

'Where?' he said, and he laid his hand on her midriff, where Jack had pulled at her jeans, as though he could sense the energy that had been there. Sometimes justice was delivered in flukes.

'Here,' she said, 'camping. Ed? Do you really love me?' It was all she could think of to avert his attention away from Jack, and from her stomach. She already knew that he did.

'What?'

'When you left in the ambulance with Steve you said you loved me.'

'I said I trust you,' he said.

Naomi ran her fingernail against the rim of the cup, staring up at the shapes of the greying clouds. They cast a moving shadow over the site.

'And I still trust you, don't I?' he said. 'I still trust you because you're mine.' He rubbed the edge of his laboured thumb against her nickel button and she could smell disinfectant on his clothing, so he'd definitely been at the hospital. He hadn't been spying all the while like the pony she'd seen in the night and she felt ill to know that her crush on Jack had been so obvious.

'Yes,' she said and she stood up, brushing invisible grass blades from her shins. 'We'd better clean up, hadn't we?'

'Know what they call Devon and Cornwall?' he said struggling after her, picking up a crushed cider can as he stood. 'The English Riviera. It's the only place in Britain warm enough to grow a palm tree! An old man who drove the taxi home from the hospital told me that. Maybe we should come here more often, rent a caravan?'

Very quickly it turned dark for a moment, pushing the hairs up on Naomi's arms. It was an evocative and mournful sensation and she knew that a cycle of her life had ended: Jack had gone. Ed was still here and Cornwall had charmed him. She'd thought she was crafty and urbane, but now she was only a strong person, capable of dealing with May's disasters.

Coney Island

Meaghan was twenty people away from the immigration desk. Her cold eyes were made crueller by the smudging kohl striped around them. They darted hopelessly round the air-conditioned airport. The Asian man at the front of the queue was arguing about goat's meat with the woman behind the glass partition. After a while he was escorted into an office for questioning and Meaghan thought she was a dead girl. But the line moved quickly along the carpet then, and she decided that she might be okay, her passport was legal after all and as far as she could tell, the leather case that she clutched with bitten, blue fingertips had not been opened. 'Don't tells them you're meeting nobody,' Denny'd said. 'Don't tells them anything. You's on holiday. And put some make-up shit on so's you look like a woman goin' on holiday. They pick you up – you's a dead girl, May.'

Through the terminal windows at the exit, the sun was beating onto the airfield like a drum roll. It was a whole different October to the one she'd left in Britain. That had only promised sleet, and a Christmas with no crepe paper or satsumas. In the women's toilet there were gaps in the formica doors, two inches wide. Anyone could see what was going on inside the cubicles, and there was nobody to look after her case, so she left it in the middle of the magnolia tiles, suspiciously watching the fat janitor through the cracked mirror to check that she didn't make off with it, or even worse, turn around and look at Meaghan. The cleaner disinfected the ceramic basins regardless, her thick braids swinging around her. She was black, not copper colour like Denny but black like the sketches of miners on the walls of Cymmer School. Meaghan's period had arrived early with the stress of attempting something illegal and international. She stuffed wads of rough, cream paper into the gusset of her knickers, which were already brown and crusted with dried blood, hoping it could somehow absorb the biting fish smell which she was surprised her own body could emit. Hesitantly, she stopped blaming Air India's food parcels for her jippy tummy.

She was seventeen and tiny, a short girl shaped like a stick. More fat on the leg of a budgie, her father used to say. She was a natural blonde (that's not to say a natural blonde was better than a suicide blonde because she'd realised a dark-eyed, exotic-looking person could be a suicide blonde, but a natural blonde could only be pale skinned and geeky, average at best). On the plane she'd dared herself to ask the airhostess for whiskey because she wanted to shake the ice around in the glass, like Denny did when he came in at the end of the day. She veered between intending to fulfil her challenge and chickening out, instead requesting fruit juice, while the glorified tea lady made her way down the aisle. Once, after a family holiday in Benidorm, her mother had suggested that Meaghan should find out about becoming an airhostess; it was a thrilling, jet setting career. 'You most certainly have the looks,' she'd said. This memory suddenly made her contemptuous of her and she did ask for whiskey.

'Scotch. Please,' she said, boldly, even though the woman was already reaching for the soft drinks. She paused, hand in the air, and then, as if remembering that her customer was always correct, she'd smiled and poured the spirit. This somehow proved Meaghan's point about the crappy job. It might be exciting to get served by a preened, big-titted airhostess but it was totally fucking boring to be the one doing the serving.

Neil Diamond's *Coming to America* was playing on the juke-box in her feverish head, the keyboard more momentous than it had ever sounded on her father's boxy record player, as though a ham-fisted kid was banging the keys with the balls of his sticky hands. For a moment she hated everything: the flight for giving her bellyache and Denny more, for making her take it. She was nervous of the long haul and of her destination, but would never admit it, and had said that morning, when he left her in Cardiff Airport, 'Tomorrow, I'll meet you on the other side of the world.' She thought it was a clever, romantic sentence but

Denny said, 'Be serious May. This is serious, this is work,' before he kissed her absently on her pale forehead. Out of the window she could see nothing but syrupy mist, still she expected Liberty to appear at any second, as she had a long time ago for all those starving Irish men. The tallest thing in Porth was the derelict Corona Pop Factory – at three storeys. It was the gateway town to the Rhondda Valley, a valley of closing down coal mines and despairing, redundant men. Not much like America, not New York at any rate, maybe a little like the Wild West, its booze-soaked old men, fighting, unshaven in the streets, old blues music pumping out of pub air vents. Ironically, Jack Daniels, the man who gave his name so proudly to Tennessee's most famous sour mash came from Treorchy, a little further up the valley, but she didn't know that just then. To live and hardly ever leave a place where the world was something that happened elsewhere, invariably meant that elsewhere was Manhattan, the setting for a million, zillion films, the setting for a real proper life. And that's where she was going, all six stone of her, alone. She wanted to crouch down on the cool, white tiles beside the lavatory and cry the sharp, devastating tears welling up like a reservoir in her throat. But that was not an option. There was only one option and it was to spring out of JFK and into America like she owned the entire motherfucking country.

'Where you goin' to honey?' The leather faced man in the driver's seat of the yellow taxi folded his fat newspaper.

Unaware that she could be described as sweet, or even soothing on a sore throat, but well aware that she was the only person in the car, she said, 'Avenue of the Americas,' and pulled the case closer to herself, holding it on her lap, protectively, like a teddy bear.

'Lady,' he said, his sun-crinkled eyes pinning her through his mirror. 'The Avenue of Americas is in central New Yawk. You want me to drive right over to Manhattan Island you gotta pay the toll charges. You gotta tell me the cross street too. That's a big avenue, what you're talkin' about.'

'It's number one thousand, two hundred and eleven,' she said, 'it's a hotel, Mid Town Hotel.'

'Say that number again,' he said.

'One two one one?' she said.

'There you go, lady,' he said. They drove into the city, the beats of other people's car radios the only sound. Along the journey, traffic began to build up around them, until the cab was just one amongst many, in an eternal, bumblebee race, overtaking and cutting each other up for no real reward. The driver's middle finger was stuck up rigid in the air, expletives jumping like beans out of his mouth. In an hour Meaghan had learned eleven new cuss words. *Jackass* was her favourite because it was playful and inoffensive. She could call Denny a jackass the next time he blew a raspberry on her mole-pocked belly. She leant her cheek against the warm glass of the window and closed her eyes, imagining his fingertips on her labia. He'd make a V sign with his fore and middle fingers and smooth it very gently against her until she moistened. Sometimes he French kissed there. She liked to lick the edges of his fingers. At Primary School her teacher had told a story in assembly about how black and white people were the same, that we all came from Africa where there was a lake in which everyone washed, to turn themselves white. The people who were still black were the people who only got there when the miraculous water was drying up, and they knelt at it with despondency, only changing the colour of the soles of their feet and palms of their hands. Denny didn't like it, but his father *was* born in Africa, in somewhere beginning with N. 'Black and white people ain't the same. May, you don't knows shit sometimes,' he said, but she still licked the places where the tones of his skin changed, like the dark parts were milk chocolate that would never run out. She liked him touching her like that and she felt her stomach flutter, just above her naval, even as she thought about it. On two occasions though, he'd reached around to her butt, and she'd worried that she'd wiped properly the last time she went to the toilet – she'd never thought of her arsehole as something sexual, only something practical, but she knew it was untainted when he rose on his knees to look at her and he'd say, 'Mm mm baby, tight ass like yours, you's worth your weight in *platinum.*'

They'd been together for five weeks. On Thursday evening, almost a week into sixth form, she'd caught a rush-hour train to Cardiff instead of walking back to the estate with Linda, her worn out navy umbrella struggling against the heavy-breathing wind, her schoolbag always smelling of rain. She was sitting in the National Express bus depot, waiting for a connection to London Bridge, her bare legs stinging beneath the hem of her plaid mini-skirt. The neon names of pubs on Mary Street blurred together in a fuzz as her eyes began to water in the chill. She flicked the pages of her biology exercise book, wondering what use that day's notes on photosynthesis would be to her on the streets of the big smoke. The family brawl she was escaping hadn't been caused by her ear piercing; it was just like the straw you pulled out of a game of *Kerplunk!* to let *all* of the glassy marbles come crashing down. She'd felt for months that her mother was growing jealous of her, which seemed somehow illogical, yet undeniable. Her father had lost his foreman job at the underwear factory and now seemed to spend most of his time at the Black Rock. Money was tight and her mother had expected her to register for the hairstyling YTS at Pontypridd Tech, but Linda wasn't going there, and during the summer Meaghan had abruptly decided that she wanted to be a veterinary surgeon, which meant she'd stay on at school, something her mother hadn't done and did not appreciate. The Saturday previous Meaghan had been to the Hannah Street jewellers with Linda, and chosen her earrings from the cotton wool-lined boxes in the glass cabinet. She danced back to the estate in the afternoon as though the shortcut path behind the Co-op was a cat-walk, feeling charming and mature. The procedure hadn't even hurt. But on arrival, instead of marvelling at the novelty, her mother clutched at Meaghan's ears, ripping one hoop out, and repeatedly calling her 'a little slut,' like she was speaking in tongues, her face plum with rage. She took the opportunity to take issue with the empty cider flagons she'd found at the bottom of the garden, and a love-bite the size and shape of a butterfly below Linda's school-shirt collar, her eyes turning into slate. At first Meaghan's thirteen year old sister Rhian had been defending Meaghan, claiming that even girls in her form had bigger sleepers, but by the end of the dumb commotion she was definitely defending their mother and the fight ended on the floor of the bedroom, Meaghan huddled beside the pleated lime valance of her bed sheet, her closest relatives beating on her folded limbs. She didn't even like cider.

Central Square emptied of its flurry until she was one of only three people left, and the daylight was fading fast. People scuttled from the station and disappeared into the black crevices of the city, their faces expressionless. When the bus came, she didn't have the verve to step on. All day she'd been sure that she would be in Piccadilly Circus by midnight, a country away from her mother, she'd purchased the ticket too. She twisted the hoops that she'd forced through the now healing holes that morning, but not even the comforting touch of the precious metal made her want to stand up. Her nerves had frayed and London seemed like the most foolish idea she'd ever dreamt up. The two other people were already opening the *South Wales Echo* on opposite sides of the coach. The elderly man at the steering wheel shrugged in his burgundy blazer but Meaghan turned her head to the timetable on the wall behind her, as though looking for another route to another place. She'd have to go *somewhere* anyway because she couldn't go back to Porth with next week's lunch money already spent. The door closed with a thump, and the bus puffed alive like something had given it mouth to mouth resuscitation. She watched the back of the huge, white vehicle prowl slowly out of the depot but sneezed as it turned the corner. When she blinked up again, her spittle cold in her fist, the bus had gone. A red sports car was parked in its place, its engine running, and waiting for her at the electric window was Denny's gold tooth smile.

She'd liked him immediately because he was from Cardiff, and had unusual eyes. Even though he was twenty-nine and maybe looked even older. His pupils were a soft, feminine brown, and the whites, not white at all but the colour of dusty piano keys.

'What you's doin' here inna rain, schoolgirl?' he'd said matter-of-factly and she hadn't answered, just smiled back wanly. He drove away and she regretted not speaking to him, but within a minute he was back, a cheeseburger, fries and a cinnamon and nutmeg ring doughnut in a brown paper bag from the Burger King on the station. 'Can I takes you some place to eat it?' he said. As she'd bent to sit in the low car, images of unsavoury things like murder shot through her mind's eye but the thought of her bloated mother stood narrow-eyed on the family doorstep was uglier. 'What's your name?' he said.

'Meaghan,' she said, spitting to feign her stamina. She was good at projecting confidence with only her voice. Her size made her a prime target for school bullies and she'd learned to speak with a nonchalance that scared people.

'May,' he said, 'I'm Denny,' and nobody had called her Meaghan since.

They went to his house in a part of the city she didn't recognise. 'Roath', he called it, to rhyme with 'fourth', and ironically, 'Porth'. It was dark by the time he indicated into the kerb and the street looked like any old terrace in the Rhondda, the houses set in blue rows and the pavement lit with whirring orange lamps. In the living room there was a black and white print of a skyscraper hung on the main wall, and the only pictures in Meaghan's were the posters in her bedroom of Jason Donovan. It was the first time she'd seen a place in which a man lived by himself. She sat politely on a leather armchair, and ate the food politely, bite by bite. She even ate the crinkle cut gherkins, closing her nose so she couldn't taste them. Denny was on the telephone where he talked mostly about a car he wanted, but would sometimes say 'yeah', in a way that seemed shorthand for things he didn't want her to hear. When they'd both completed these activities and there was nothing left to do but look at one another, he said, 'You seems to be's in some kind of trouble May, so stay tonight if you want.' She looked blankly at him, so he elaborated. 'On the settee I's mean, I don't gives my bed to nobody.'

She did stay but for most of the night, could not sleep. Hours were punctuated by waking thoughts of Rhian having to explain to the form tutor that her sister did not go home the night before. When she woke at ten o'clock, Denny had gone but there was a twenty pound note crumpled like rubbish on the corner of the coffee table nearest to her. She went to the window and peered out through the blind at the unfamiliar street. There was a tattoo parlour on the opposite side with highly detailed dragon designs posted on the smeared glass, next door to an exotic pet shop. She didn't want to leave and have to navigate her way back to the city centre in her sweaty school uniform as it would be obvious to the people she passed that she was some sort of problem child, bunking. She knew also that if she stayed, her mother would never find her, could never pin her down to that address, so she went back to the settee and slept some more, only venturing into the kitchen to steal a two-finger Kit Kat from a biscuit barrel beside the electric kettle, and two further visits to the window, where the snake tanks in the pet shop display became less strange and more exciting. When Denny returned, expecting never to see the girl or the money again, he found them both, like ornaments, in their same places.

Meaghan lost her virginity that night. After Denny'd fed her a Burger King again, that time without a doughnut for dessert, they'd sat on the settee and watched quiz shows on the television, passing a lit joint back and forth as though it was a heavy object which neither of them wanted to hold up for too long. They talked about chemistry, the only subject he'd passed, he said, and he talked slow and easy; not trying too hard, which boys her own age did; their hands moving in before they'd finished their sentences. She was very stoned by the time he carried her to the bedroom and stripped her. It took him forty-five minutes in all to penetrate her, repeatedly humping his lithe body against her spongy pink skin, his shaved head hard and smooth against her face. When she did split it wasn't painful, her exhausted body only seemed to flood with a numbing sensation like needles and pins and she slept easily, naked, above the damp and musty duvet. The next day was Saturday and he drove her to town to buy a wardrobe's worth of new things from Dorothy Perkins on Queen Street, including dainty satin French knickers and padded lace bras, not at all like her father used to make. He fingered multicolour notes from a roll of money in his jeans pocket. Meaghan had never imagined that life could be so simple without parental guidance. She sensed vaguely that she had experienced some type of loss, but had no idea that Denny might have added to it. He was her sexy, rich rescuer and she was already in love.

'That'll be $45,' the taxi driver said, screeching into the side-walk, an elderly woman with a miniature poodle jumping out of their way. 'And a tip, honey,' he said. Meaghan reached into the cup of her bra where the skin of her breast was clammy and pulled out a hundred dollar note. It looked fake, like something from a board game, the words, *In God We Trust*, printed on its green face. 'Thank you,' he said, taking it with his scissor fingers, 'you have a nice day.' Meaghan stood on the pavement with her prized case and watched him disappear into one of the four lanes clogged with identical cars. She'd been anxious that some hard-faced, thick-skinned New Yorker would instantly see that she was a seventeen year old country bumpkin and fleece her before she left the airport. Her fear was now fully realised.

In the hotel, the receptionist was smiling but not looking at her, the pearl pink lipstick line around her mouth overstated so it pouted out like it was stung, the way the girls who gathered sometimes in Denny's hallway looked naturally. 'Help you?' she said, without it parting.

'Meaghan Davies,' Meaghan said, 'from Wales. I have a room booked.'

'You mean you have a reservation, Ma'am, no problem.' She rang a bell on the marble counter inattentively. 'You want help, honey,' she said and nodded at a boy mincing across the polished, oil coloured lobby floor in a red jacket and white trousers, like an entertainer from Barry Island Butlin's. He curtsied before Meaghan and reached to take her case out of her hands. Meaghan's grip immediately tightened, so they were both yanking at either handle, Meaghan's teeth clenched, until the bellboy pranced backward. He peered at the receptionist in panic and she looked at Meaghan over her steel nail file.

'Do you want him to carry the bag or not Missy?' she said miserably.

Meaghan followed the boy to the lift and watched the floors below her evaporate. On the landing he swiped her door-card and rushed into the room to whip the curtains open. He laid the case on the bed, exaggerating care, and waited stiffly at the door.

'How much?' Meaghan said.

'How much you think.'

She took five dollars from her damp wad of paper and put it into the boy's eager hand. As his jaw swelled gleefully she guessed that it was too much. She waved him away disappointedly. If Denny were there he'd laugh at her, or swear.

She sat gently on the bed, beside the case, her legs crossed uncomfortably, and stared at it guardedly as though she expected it to explode and burn her face, like fat from a sizzling frying pan. The white piping around its edges turned beige under her gaze, the Sinatra lyric about making it there, making it anywhere repeating itself until she was deaf to the traffic outside. After an hour, she noticed the out of focus umbrella plant in the corner of her vision and she began to hope that it was real.

She needed a chemist and so had to leave the hotel. On the forty second street sidewalk her pointed chin was aimed at the ground, her eyes flitting in one or other direction like her old Bionic Woman doll did when she'd flicked a switch on its plastic back. It was as though resting her eyes on any given object could physically harm her, and Mid Town Manhattan appeared to buzz cacaphonically. She walked so fast she actually passed two pharmacies without realising it, wondering what American's called tampons, her thighs sweating so her jeans stuck to them, the hair follicles there itching impatiently. Three blocks away from the rotating hotel door she'd acclimatised to the heat and the stampede around her. A man tried to pull her aside and sell his watch and she flapped away without registering him. The area was sleazy and dangerous. Prostitutes leant against walls running their hands up and down their fishnets. Neon lights advertised *Live Sex Shows* and grimy men huddled in groups baring their rotting teeth. Even the graffiti was intimidating; unlike the childish words scrawled behind the Co-op, it was masculine, secretive and violent. She looked at the sky, hoping it could provide some form of escape and saw an electronic Coca Cola billboard on the side of a building, the green bottle continually tilting and pouring its sugary contents and suddenly she halted, recognising her surroundings.

On the first day of every New Year she and Rhian had sat on the velveteen sofa, sick of turkey, the holiday becoming laborious while a newscaster presented celebrations from around the world. In Trafalgar, drunken people jumped into the freezing fountains and here, in Times Square, people were crushed. She whirled around to look at the advertisements above her in astonishment. One of the tramps dropped an item onto his lit oil drum fire and ash floated in the air for a moment, like snow. Rhian would never believe it. In Porth, watching the television screen, it had seemed to her and Rhian as though these multicoloured people living amongst tall buildings had zilch to do with their own lives. Meaghan had never expected a black boyfriend, or to go to New York and she'd only bought a bus ticket to London because that's what runaways on Coronation Street did. From a young age she'd only expected to spend her days dodging the rain and even her craziest dreams only took her as far as cutting dog's claws and neutering stray cats. Abetting major crime had never been part of her plan. She sensed people beginning to notice her and ran back the way she had come. On her way out of a drugstore close to the hotel she passed a Dunkin' Donuts counter and was contemplating a girl her age working there, thinking that she might be next year's Madonna when an aggravated hiss of steam rising from a drain caught her. There, on the other side of the street, a swarm of people, a herd of cattle with fat arms, legs and torsos but no distinguishable features hurried out of a station, marching towards her, no attention to the Walk/Don't Walk signals, just a big school of flesh, moving. On the pavement at their feet, a boy crouched over his bleeding friend. 'Help me,' he said, she could lipread the words. 'Help us, we need medical attention here.' Nobody looked down. Nobody helped them. And Meaghan turned and walked into the hotel lobby, the sick, sweet food and rubbish smell of the city caught in her mouth.

Next day, New York woke up in the soundtrack of a movie, police sirens and fire engines attending human and natural disasters, bin men clearing, Fed Ex men delivering. Meaghan jumped from her sleep, fumbling into the case she'd shared her bed with, her hair matted in fine, wet, yellow knots. Under the poor light she felt the plastic cases of the money lined like bricks under the cotton T-shirts. She relaxed. She studied Denny's map, planning her journey. Get on the orange F train at forty-second and exit at Stillwell Avenue. 'The easiest thing you ever did,' Denny'd said and she remembered she hadn't liked the way he said it in past tense, as if money running was the only reason he needed her. For half a second she allowed herself to consider keeping the case but she wouldn't know where to go, or how to change the sterling to dollars. Outside it was still scorching for October. She did what a New York tourist should never do. She looked up, again. The sun was obscured by a skyscraper – the Empire State, she thought it might have been, the sky azure. Underground, it was cool. Morning shipments of the *New York Times* sat at entrances to news stores that sold candy instead of chocolate and bagels instead of sandwiches. She'd never been on a subway, not even on the London Underground. The annual school trip to Madam Tussaud's used a 58-seat coach from Pontypridd which dropped her back at her front door on a Friday evening. She queued at the booth for tokens to Brooklyn, the case weightier by the minute. One of a group of black and Puerto Rican boys flipping tokens on the slate floor approached her, landing an inch from the end of her nose.

'Whyn't you buy one a' my tokens girly?' He flexed his gold shoulder muscles and they pushed out his basketball vest. 'Cost you fifty cents; you keep waiting for that nigger bitch sell you one, cost you two dollars.' Meaghan liked the healthy sweat scent of the boy and tried to convey it by rolling her eyes over him lustfully. He spoke back to the others in furious Spanish but stared all the while at one of her earrings. She already knew how it would feel to get it ripped out so she turned to the woman in the booth, pretending not to have heard him. 'Crazy fuckin' limey,' he said eventually like he'd read it off a tattoo on her forehead and walked away to kick balls of rat shit onto the track below him.

Near Greenwood Cemetery where the train rose above ground and the heat began to smack on the windows, a Latino teenager wailed with the inaudible music in her headphones, her eyes screwed tight in application. There were no white people left on the train. Meaghan began to read the adverts facing her. One urged her to report any murders of police officers she might have witnessed in order to claim her thousand dollar reward, the words bold and black, and the background white and splattered with pretend blood spots.

She began to wonder if Denny had ever killed a police officer.

Life in Roath had become as routine as her school timetable. Denny was hardly ever there. At first she thought he worked in a bank because he handled money like it would never run out, throwing his change around the house like worthless button badges. Her uncle who had worked at the Royal Mint in Llantrisant never picked coins up from the floor because at work he was forbidden to do it and gradually he forgot their value. But she realised one day that Denny only ever left the house in casual clothing, in denim and Egyptian cotton that probably cost as much as a work suit. While he was out she watched MTV and ate Mars Bars, her legs hooked over the arm of the settee. One time she got so bored she thought about asking the shop across the road how much it would be to put one of those big Chinese dragons down her hip, surprise Denny. When he was there she made chicken sandwiches and brewed tea. 'You's gonna get off that cute ass of yours one day?' he'd said, seemingly for no reason, on a stormy Monday evening, and that's what she'd done to impress him, forcing the bag against the side of the mug until clouds of ginger fluid burst out like paint from a brush dipped in white spirit. He never thanked her for it but he never complained, so she repeated the task three times a week, always cold chicken and sweet tea. Every Saturday there was seventy or eighty pounds on the table, and he'd say, 'Get something black,' or 'Get something red,' or 'Girly this week May, get some flowery shit, you're gettin' to look too old too quick.'

On the third week there'd been an IRA bomb-scare on Western Avenue and she returned early to find the house full with Asian women. Bengali, Denny'd called them later. They were laughing when she opened the door and dressed in good trouser suits with thick shoulder pads. Matt lipstick and expensive foundation, but their eyes were sad, as though they were attending a funeral and the glamour was something required, not actually enjoyed. Denny was standing in the centre of the room and they were looking at him with admiration and fear.

'Look,' he said, 'this is my baby,' placing his hands on Meaghan's shoulders like she was his child. 'My baby May,' and the women eyed her with half-hearted sympathy.

That night she'd been in bed wearing her something red, when she heard raised voices from downstairs.

'She can't works no more Den,' somebody was saying, 'she's four months' gone.'

'Half my girls works four, five, seven months' gone.' That was Denny, giggling.

'But that's not what I want. I wants to look after her proper and the big shops in town, they got cameras and shit now, I can't earn no more.'

For a while there was a throbbing silence. Then Denny's voice piped up coldly. He sounded like her mother.

'The way I see's it Fab, you's not working, your girl not working, you don't needs no shooter. Leave it here and you can pays me a pound a week outta ya dole. You must thinks I'm a fucking clown. Do I looks like a fucking clown?'

A minute or so later the front door slammed so all of the other doors in the house shuddered. Meaghan thought that Denny had left the house with whoever else had been downstairs because two cars started up in the street. She waited for six or seven minutes, watching the green numbers flick over on the digital video recorder before tip-toeing down, missing the tread on the bottom because it creaked. There was a handgun on the table which looked so shiny and small she thought it had to be a toy. Denny was perched on the sofa, his legs wide open, grinning so the light bulb caught the metal in his teeth.

A boy and a girl a little younger than Meaghan were snogging at the far end of the clacking carriage and she couldn't avert her eyes. The simple, tranquil manner in which the boy's fingers danced on the plastic seat beside him, and the flashes of their purple tongues made her feel abandoned. She stared at the girl's striped scarf. It was the same colour as her school tie and she wondered if Linda had stayed with Tomos, the boy who'd bitten her neck, or if she'd moved onto James, the boy who sat at the top of the canteen, and whose eyes they felt move across the tables with the smell of burnt vegetables and Dettol. For the first time, she missed the Rhondda and she tried to quell its dragging sensation, telling herself that she was lucky, that she had gained freedom, but she was clutching the leather case against her chest as though it were human, and she realised that all she had was money.

The authentic Coney Island was a fun fair on the Brooklyn coast, surrounded on three sides by the Atlantic Ocean. The amusements were closed but the acrid smell of holiday food, of pretzels and hot dogs and floss was still as strong as it had ever been. She strolled along the wide boardwalk towards it, her jacket too thick for the bright weather, the sun turning the sands of Brighton Beach white hot. On the benches in front of the bodegas, eccentric ladies sat in black hats and clothes, speaking Russian, squashed-faced terriers at their heels. Men played chess contests that had been going on all year. As she turned into the entrance behind the aquarium she noticed Ronald Reagan's face had been cut messily out of the *National Enquirer* and sellotaped to a target in the shooting gallery. Everything seemed too quiet.

The counterfeit Coney Island was a fun-fair in Porthcawl, where a younger boy from her school had been killed on the faulty water chute. By that point she and Rhian hadn't been there for years, but while her grandparents were alive they'd been there every bank holiday, the salt from the sea and their chips thick in their nostrils. She didn't understand now why one was real and one was false. The New York version wasn't any grander than the Welsh one. In the 20's it had been the height of sophistication, where the wealthy people spent their dollars, but that veneer had been eaten into.

She waited next to the Ferris wheel, as Denny had told

her, spying around the fairground at the colourful graffiti. Through the cage fence a man passed on the pavement with a ghetto blaster wedged into his shoulder and for a breath the fair was alive but the music soon faded and all she heard was a breeze and an electrical current from a forgotten television. There was a sour-faced man sitting in a caretaker booth, his little eyes screwing into her under the shadow of his baseball cap but when she returned the glare he looked away. She'd been there for ten minutes when she noticed another person standing beside the fastened fortune teller kiosk, watching her, his ragged drainpipe jeans ripped to reveal bruised skin. She looked at the floor and began to bite her nails, stretching her foot out to kick the case closer to herself. She listened very hard but could not hear the women gossiping in Russian. The man in the booth was still watching her.

Time passed slowly but soon she saw another man, a short Puerto Rican smoking, one hairy arm resting on the gate, and the sun melted away to Manhattan island so everything turned frosty and sinister and she began to feel like Dorothy, hanging around in the enchanted castle when the evil wheelies were about to attack. She lifted her hand to glance at her watch, dead on eleven, he'd said, but hit something fleshy with her elbow. The grey-haired man beside her wore a white kaftan. He was so tall he was painful to look at and she stopped short of his chest, uncertain that she even wanted to see what was in his eyes. He said nothing but edged up to her, his thick, worn skin almost touching the erect blonde hair of her neck. He smelt of coconut and Meaghan hated it. She stepped away, dragging the case along the concrete ground but just as easily he sidled closer, touching her. She flinched before she could move again, sure that she was about to die; in Coney Island of all places, like the boy from her school. She'd never smuggle arms out of America via Canada and land back in Cardiff unscathed, not to tell the tale. Her life would be extinguished in a bloody fairground.

Promptly, fifty thousand pounds seemed like very little and she was going to kick it at the hippy next to her and run like a wilderbeast toward the water. Her adrenaline was bursting through her veins, when she saw Denny casually coming toward her from the sidewalk side of the fair. The man next to her saw this too and he stood away where she could see his kindly face.

'You're a very, very lucky gal,' he said, and around her the strangers scattered like crows. The man laughed with an abstract, ambiguous chuckle and walked slowly away, his hands in his pockets. It was only then that she began to shake.

'What's the matter May?' Denny said, tutting as he retrieved his money, gladly throwing the bag over his shoulder. 'Let's go buy some guns.'

Valley Lines

Caitlin didn't know what to say to the gaggle of rubber-masked kids on her doorstep. Oh it was an impressive display, no doubt about it. A lime green latex Frankenstein with the bolts in its head, dull and rust tinged. But it smacked of money, an abundance of money, and a bored lack of creativity. It wasn't that long ago she came home one autumn and plastered her whole face in her mother's No.7 green eye shadow, then back combed her hair into four big knots. She'd known it was the right way to do it when she got up to Chepstow Road and her Auntie hadn't recognised her, just put twenty pence in her basket and closed the door on her face. And all the other kids were still in Spar choosing their cheap, plastic witches' hats. Somehow, this memory made her superior to the children and she rose on the balls of her feet so she was taller than the ghost at the back.

'Trick or treat,' the impatient little cow in the bridal veil said, again.

Trick or treat, an impudent American phrase. Not the 'Please help Mari Llwyd', the upper Rhondda Fawr people were saying when she was ten or eleven. But then in Welsh Folk Culture at Sixth Form College she'd learned that the Mari Llwyd was a rotting horse skull the peasants traipsed round on New Year's Eve, scaring people into sharing their whiskey. It was a whole wad of mixed up, nonsensical bollocks in the end. She gave the Frankenstein a two pound coin and then, as they were skipping away, she said, 'It's not Halloween until tomorrow.' She couldn't understand the parents, leaving their kids out on cold winter nights during an age of murder and paedophilia, not the funny, old pervert in the pine end who likes looking at little pairs of white knickers anymore, it's nurses and caretakers and teachers, lethal injections administered to new born babies and frail eight year old girls, buggered and incinerated. Then a jolt of terror struck through her thorax as she looked at the clock, 9pm, Sunday night. A thousand bath times raced through her mind, a thousand sleepless nights she'd spent wrestling with the onslaught of another school week, five days of intimidation, torture, humiliation, all because she wasn't five feet yet. But then she remembered, and relaxed, slumped her adult form back into the lumpy settee and picked up the Merlot. It was only work.

Work. Early on a Monday morning the fat, black Cardiff city crows were still asleep. The air was part frost from the cold, part beer hops from the brewery near the station. Caitlin walked through the Grangetown area, narrow eyed and shivering, following her silvery breath towards Sloper Road. At the job centre on the corner a man in an army parka with a clump of ginger hair leant against the door, his stolen litter tongs thrust through the letterbox, fervently picking at two brown envelopes lying face down on the horse hair mat. He stopped as Caitlin walked past, whistling through his teeth. She turned her head towards the empty main road and fingered the cotton strap of her handbag.

When she turned the key to her unit in a vast warehouse behind the Ninian Park football ground, the steadfast, acrid smell of developing fluid waved out into the murky corridor. She remembered going home to her teenage bedroom from a one night stand to find her mother had emptied the contents of every last bottle of Amyl Nitrate into the sink. Sixteen bottles she'd bought with a cheque her father sent from London to pay for an Austrian school skiing trip, but she'd told her mother it wasn't poppers.

'It's not drugs Mam, you silly bitch. It's developing fluid for my photography course. Jesus Christ, why are you so thick? That's fifty quid's worth of educational material gone to waste. I'm not on drugs, am I?' Because parents knew virtually nothing about narcotics you could tell them any old shit. She threw her coat over the chair. This was her work: developing still images, mostly for Peter Dukowski, the odd yet refined Polish man with a studio on City Road, sometimes for Peter Williams, a school photographer with a penchant for farting the tunes to

Beatles love songs. On slow days she tended to the machine which developed holiday snaps of the general, hopeless public, a machine she'd nick named Dennis Hopper. It was a working life spent looking into the faces of strangers. In the darkroom she emptied Friday's water trays under the minimal orange bulb, carefully lifting the paper and not scratching the images with the teeth of her tongs. The smile of a flush and buxom bride. The proud and padded shoulders of a mother with a son in graduation cloak. The glazed and naive eyes of a small child. And then she hung them up to dry.

It was raining on the way home and she had no umbrella, just drizzle. The wind was worse, slapping at her suede calves but the damage would be the same; thirty minutes sweat and arm ache underneath her hairdryer. The tiled floor of the railway station was coated in rain water. Trainer and court shoe soles left dirty trails of footsteps inside it. Up on the platform it was starting to get dark. At primary school she'd had nightmares about walking home alone in the darkness. She prayed that school hours would never clash with Daylight Saving Time because she'd dreamt of the consequences and praying was easier even though God was something like a giant white lop-eared rabbit. Now it gave her a purpose, a kind of Protestant work ethic – never seeing winter sunshine, that was good. When the train came she couldn't see it for raincoats and briefcases, fingers wrapped tight around the handles, skin turning blue. She didn't have the weight or the insolence to push forward so she hoped it was the Tonypandy and followed the herd in half footsteps, up the stairs and into the carriage. She leant her head against the window as the engine bubbled up, then sat up straight again. She couldn't see Spiderman. *Spiderman*; that's what she'd called him since she spied the comic in his record bag; up and down the aisle, no Spiderman. Perhaps he'd had an accident. Maybe she should call the Royal Glamorgan, or the University hospital. She could feel the outline of her mobile telephone through the cotton of her bag. Wait. No. That was completely absurd. She didn't even know his real name.

The day's last light projected into the room, diffused by the sheet tacked to the rotting window frame. The first thing Iolo saw through his squint was a pop-up internet window, a pornographic image, two men, cocoa colour skin, and erect penises. He rolled to the edge of the settee, switched the lap-top computer off at the mains and rolled back to the fold where the seat cushions ended and the other cushions began. He closed his eyes. 'Shit,' he said after a minute. His voice floated in the air for a moment, then disappeared into the gloom. 'Shit. Fuck. Shit.' Reality poured in through his ear canals. It was Monday. It was late afternoon. He'd slept through a whole work day. He was in trouble. But there was nothing to get up for now. He stayed, restrained in his cold, urinous sweat, paralysed by the side effects of amphetamine sulphate and wondered how much profit he'd lost by hoovering up his own drugs. Then the gay porn came back to his mind and he wondered if those Berlin punks had any idea how hard they had affected him, screaming at a little eleven year old kid across a busy

Charlottenburg High Street. 'Little English fucker. Little military cock sucker. Gay. *Ja, besimmt,*' their harsh German accents grating on him. He wasn't even English. He kept his mouth shut, his tongue wedged up tight against the ridges on the roof of his mouth and he swallowed all of the saliva it produced in quick succession, mouthful after mouthful. But it was no barrier. He was going to have to get up and be sick.

On the way back from the bathroom, the aftertaste of his stomach acids burning the soft pulp of his gums, he flicked the severe bare bulb on. A postcard hung in the letterbox like a stick in a dog's mouth. Marbella; another fucking beach, another fucking palm tree. 'Mum and I are enjoying ourselves as ever, trust you are too. Mum still waiting for you to visit.' His father was such a petulant arsehole – bought all that Queen and Country bullshit, called his only son Iolo. Nobody in South Wales would dream of calling their son Iolo, as Iolo discovered when he moved there, age fifteen. *Trust you are too.* Yeah, right Dad. He didn't so much throw the card, as drop it, but it skimmed on the fusty air, like a pebble and landed on the coffee table with the drugs and the records and the comics and the porn. He pulled his trousers on, the synthetic sliding up the skin of his legs. Outside it was black and cold. Nobody ever came to sweep the falling leaves from the sycamores lining the road. Now it'd rained and they'd turned to mulch, they didn't even crunch under his trainers. On the corner of the next block two men were laughing loudly, one wearing a black cloak, his face caked in white make-up, the other in a beret holding a crude plastic machine gun. 'Iolo', Iolo thought one of them said, so Iolo walked towards them. They looked at him, their ridiculous faces full of confusion. A train shuddered past on the railway bridge above, vibrating in the ground under their feet. All three men looked up towards the row of yellow lit square windows speeding through the sky. Once the train disappeared the men walked away, laughing again when they got to the other side of the road. Iolo shrugged his shoulders as though he wasn't embarrassed or dizzied by this misunderstanding. Either drugs had taken his hearing away or someone was taking the piss. A fat Asian woman in the shop with the purple awning sold him ten cigarettes and a big banana milkshake. Back at the house he took his weighing scales out of the gas cupboard, swept the loose grains of speed from the table, directing it all with his hands into the balancing pan. He wrapped the grams in the pages of a worthless Batman fanzine, licked his fingers and made off for an evening of trade at Pontypridd Student Union.

Cailtin was standing at the bakery in the supermarket. Fairy cakes with black spider webs iced across the surface were down to half price. She looked at the doughnuts for a whole three minutes, shifting her weight from her heels to her toes and back again. Seventy-nine pence for ten, hardly expensive but she only wanted one, maybe two. To buy an individual doughnut cost fifty pence but they were dry under the light and the icing sugar had worn away. She should buy the whole bag, she should, but eight would go to waste, another eight doughnuts in the rubbish bin. If she'd thought about it yesterday she could have given last week's to the Halloween kids, that'd teach the cheeky sods. It was stupid really; she didn't even like doughnuts, only the jam in the middle. The dough was so heavy and tasteless it was a relief to get to the jam. The jam was so good you could forgive the dough. Just like life of course. It knocked ten shades of shit out of you before it gave you anything to smile about. And buying a pot of jam, that was just cheating. She picked the pink paper bag up by its handle with her forefinger, looking at it like a turd she'd fished out of the litter tray, and then she dropped it in her basket.

It didn't rain on Tuesday but the air was crisp and chilled. Iolo stood on Central station, another fruitless day at a windowless shop on Cowbridge Road behind him. Selling wasn't really the verb, raw throatily explaining why the *Viz* 1991-96 collection is utterly valueless, why they're never going to be valuable, maybe. Assuring, voice trembling, a twelve year old child and his grandmother that the second edition of *Tank Girl* really is worth 2K, and no, he couldn't possibly take it out of the plastic bag and show them. A knuckle wrapping from his Chinese boss who thinks he's lazy. 'Lazy, lazy fukka.' Comics, Jesus, he couldn't imagine what possessed him to take the job. He turned away from the crowd on the platform and ripped the Velcro open on his record bag, took a peek, checked it was still there; a 1967 *Denis the Menace*. Sell it on e-bay; it's a three month supply of disco biccies, sorted. He slouched against the waiting room wall and lit a cigarette, the nicotine scratching his inflamed mouth. He staved a cough. Then he saw her. Her face first, hovering in mid air, her body obscured by other commuters. She wasn't happy today, she was tired, tired from a day doing whatever it was she did. When she looked at him he dropped his cigarette, stamped on it vehemently, his interest in tobacco immediately vanished. He stood up straight again, taking his weight back from the red brick wall. He opened his arms, ever so slightly, and held his shoulders still, awkwardly, in mid shrug.

Caitlin smiled tight lipped at Spiderman. He was standing motionless at the front of the platform, his face another ambiguous expression. This time he raised his eyebrows so his eyeballs widened and wrinkles appeared in his forehead. Her mother would have called them Valley Lines, like laughter lines, but caused by stress, strife, poverty, alcohol, drugs, chain-smoking; anything a Welsh person endured in order to stay alive, pessimistic old cow, her mother. The train screamed into the station and she followed Spiderman to the carriage. Valley Lines, it said on a map in front of her. She sat opposite him in the seats that faced one another, tried not to appear rude, stared out of the window and scanned back to him while his eyes were closed, his mind concentrating as hard as it could on the beat in his plug-in earphones. He sat with his legs wide open, his bag on his lap, his arms clutched tight around it. She could smell the smoke and alkaline scent. His grey hair was clipped close to his skull, black grey in some parts, white grey in others. Her uncle was grey at a young age, perhaps that's what she saw in him, her benevolent uncle who saved her from her jealous aunt and all her pedantic questions. 'Got your swimming badge yet? Writing your S's the right way round yet?' Her uncle'd take her to the garden and show her the frog in the pond; he knew he'd married a bitch. She tried to remember when she'd first noticed Spiderman, if it was any sort of significant date, but she couldn't, he just gradually streamed into her consciousness, maybe a year ago, maybe less. She thought about asking him where he was yesterday, and at the same time she knew that she never would. It was nosey, intrusive, all those things she despised. Besides, for all she knew he might not even speak English, his answer could come out in silver-tongued Italian. And, oops, too late, they were stopping at Pontyridd station. Spiderman gathered up his stuff, picked his thick, athletic legs over the middle aged fat woman next to him, looked at Caitlin, just for a second while he waited for the door to slide open then he jumped from the train.

She was there again on Thursday. Of course she was, she was there everyday. Everyday he could remember shuffling his aching muscles and rotting skin back to the stale Broadway bed-sit, she was there. Except for a week in spring when he'd wondered what had kept her away, influenza, hay-fever, a holiday with a girlfriend or a boyfriend in Spain. He'd worried it was Meningitis even, because she was young, because she might have lived in close proximity to other young people, she might have lived in a shared house. Anyway, he worried, knowing he had no right to worry, no right to assume, until she came back, her face more coloured, her eyes refreshed and he enjoyed her silent company again. The platform was almost empty. The retail people stayed in the city, overtime for late night

Christmas shopping. Christmas – what a soul crushing concept. The girl was standing right in front of him, her tiny frame wrapped in black faux fur. He could see right down onto the crown of her dyed red hair, right down into the dark roots where her skin would be hot. She turned around suddenly and he thought she'd berate him for staring. She always knew when he was staring, perhaps all women did. No, that couldn't be true or else they'd never get followed and raped. But she just rolled her eyes. The train was two minutes late and he sucked air over his teeth, quietly, in sympathy with her.

The vibration of the wheels on the track jarred in Caitlin's head. She could hear Spiderman's breath next to her. It was almost comfortable. But somebody'd left a window open further up on the carriage. The cold brought water to her eyes but she wouldn't walk there and close it. It'd be heavy for her and the people watching would smirk. She hoped the bald man nearest would close it but he was oblivious to everything except the *Echo* he held close to his face. Near Taff's Well bridge she saw the outline of a boy in the darkness. Just one boy, on his own, his arms up-stretched menacingly. Instantly she knew the omen was ill, like a cow who knows in its stomach when the slaughter man has arrived. When she was four she watched a man fall off a motorbike and die, and she knew he'd die. The outer glass on a window on the opposite side of the carriage shattered. None of it fell out; it just crumbled like a burning sheet of paper. The woman sitting next to it stood up quickly, looked around and moved away. Then the lights went out and someone gasped. The brakes shrieked. And the train stopped. She knew her body was jerking forward but she couldn't feel it. Her feet were still flat on the floor. She heard her head hit the steel bar. She only heard it thud, her head was numb and something soft but heavy pulled her back to the seat and held her there, unable to move until the florescent yellow light came back. Superman, no, Spiderman.

Iolo didn't know what he was doing, or what he would do next, he only knew that behind the small time drug dealer persona, behind the petty thief persona, he was a decent human being. And the girl had hurt herself. He held his hand tight around her tiny forearm on some strange automatic pilot device he'd never known he possessed. She looked at him, bug eyed.

'You okay?' he said.

'Yeah,' she said, 'I bumped my head.' She tried to move her arm, to lift it and touch her forehead, check it was still there, or feel the size of the lump, but he was holding it down between their laps. The train started again, the revving of the engine shaking the carriage and replacing the dumb silence. The other people on the train eyeballed the smashed window and swore with contempt at a nation of bored youths. None of them noticed that Iolo was holding this strangers hand, only him. He noticed. He noticed so hard the touch was burning his skin, but he didn't let go. The girl shook her head and her red curls flailed this way and that. Her hair seemed to get redder by the minute. She sat forward and looked out of the window at the Pontypridd station marker, then looked back at him, but he didn't let go. Nobody got on and nobody got off and then she seemed to relax, sit back, stop sweating. Iolo relaxed too, squinted out of the window at the black scenery; he'd never been here before.

'This is my stop,' Caitlin said and she stood up quickly, forcefully, her arm still attached to Spiderman. He nodded compliantly and followed her, his robust legs slow after the journey. He let her hand slip free as they stepped off the train and he looked at his hand as though it was something he'd lost and found again after a long time, his fingers outstretched enough for her to see the webbing between them. Right up close to his face. For a moment she'd thought he would murder her. Think of the worst case scenario, she'd told herself, and a snuff movie she'd seen at college came into her head. Somewhere about him there was a machete, and he'd take her to a park under the pretence of fucking her. Central Park she was thinking, although she knew she was in Wales, and he'd cut her tits off instead, leave her there to bleed. Something in his eyes told her this was ridiculous. He smiled at her like an amused baby. He didn't have words, leave alone violence. They were walking through Tonypandy subway, racism daubed on the walls. She wanted to tell him that she'd like to live in the city, that this place was stifling her, but then he'd ask her why she didn't and she'd have to explain that she didn't have the social skills, that she couldn't make friends in this close knit community so how was she going to do it in a multi-nationality capital city. As if he hadn't already realised all this. And then she thought about her underwear, all the lace and silk and Lycra she had in her knicker drawer and she just happed to be wearing cotton, white cotton.

Iolo knew it was her house when she stopped walking and looked at him speechless, her skin shining orange under a street lamp, a two bedroom terrace. For a second he thought she'd offer him coffee and he hoped she didn't because he wouldn't know what to say. He didn't like coffee. For a bisexual man, he wasn't that keen on sex. But she didn't speak. She fell weightlessly onto his chest, wormed her arms around his waist. He stayed like that for a while, letting her hug him, the chapel at the end of the street looking at him aggressively. She smelt of chemicals. He wondered how he could end this, how he could walk away from her and look her in the face again tomorrow night, and how, if he didn't walk away, would it turn out? How could she change the disgusting, pointless life of drugs, clubs and loneliness he'd carved out for himself? She'd worked her face up to his shoulder and kissed his neck, sucked on his earlobe, his silver stud lolling about on her tongue.

'Stop,' he said and he pushed her away, but then in the lamp he saw the folds in her full lips shining under their gloss and he took her face in his hands, kissed her warm, wet mouth, curled his tongue into every bitter cavity, his hands pressed flat on her midriff, her hands working up into his T-shirt, and it felt good. Oh, and, no. No, she couldn't make him wholesome, couldn't make him watch TV, wear slippers, wash their car on Sunday. She couldn't make him straight, she couldn't change anything. You take yourself wherever you go. He'd only make her miserable. But perhaps if they were friends, she could make him a little less forlorn. He took his tongue out of her mouth.

'I can't. I think I'm gay,' Spiderman said, in a voice without accent, his face plain and bland, no character, another ambiguous half stare. Caitlin looked in his eyes for humour, for a glimmer of a joke but all she saw was the red rash around them, the amphetamine residue.

'Okay,' she heard herself say, 'that's good because I'm wearing really ugly knickers.' She breathed deep, her winded lungs begging for oxygen and Spiderman laughed. He stood in the street laughing at her, his mouth playful. Despite herself, she smiled back, managed a short, sharp giggle then she put the key in the front door.

'Wait,' he said to her back, and she half turned to him. 'What's your name?'

'Caitlin,' she said. 'What's yours?'

'Iolo.'

'Iolo?'

'Yeah. Very uncool, I know. And Welsh.'

'No, it's nice,' she said and she turned around, stepping back into the street. He was dancing on the spot, tiptoeing away, backwards. 'What's the thing with comics? You follow women home, but you're gay. You're thirty years old but you have a Spiderman comic in your bag.'

He didn't answer but he laughed heartily again. 'How come you're so short?' he said. 'You're so short and you smell like a chemist.'

'Yeah,' she said, shrugging her shoulders, unconcerned, the corners of her mouth drawing up again.

'See you tomorrow,' he said, and he waved and walked away.

Caitlin sighed, watched him go. Then she opened the front door, ran to the bathroom, washed the tobacco out of her mouth with cold water and in the mirror, calmly inspected her purply bruise.

Merry Go-Rounds

It started in a club. It was Valentine's Day. The singer of
the band was a small sinewy man in pink leather trousers
with a pink cotton T-shirt. His tattoos were slipping out of
his sleeves. His hair was long and wavy, and thinning at the
fringe. After one song he took his T-shirt off and hung by
his defined arms from the steel rafter. His feet swung out
in front of him. He was strong. I could see the worn soles
of his basketball boots. Behind him, three other men carved
electric decadence into the dry ice with drum rolls and
tricky guitar chords. After two songs the man in pink was
singing in falsetto while women stripped away his trousers.
Underneath them there was a zebra print leotard. The
crowd arced out around the stage. After three songs he
scissor kicked into the ether and landed on the floor in
front of me, his Les Paul held up in the air, his brown eyes

rolled back into his head. His cheekbones stood out of his skin like silver bruises. Around him, the floor was a sheet of raised terracotta tiles, like a giant bar of ceramic chocolate. He picked himself up off it and smiled at me with thick lips. I swallowed what remained of the crisp beer in my glass bottle.

'Wiry bastard i'n' 'e?' John bellowed into my ear, spraying saliva over my neck. 'That's the future, what you're looking at. It's like Freddie Mercury on helium.'

'John, you prick,' I said, 'you just fuckin' spat all over me. Go and get me another drink.'

'Yeah,' he shouted above the music, nodding like a toy dog, 'I know. I'm serious though. Think about it Amber; this band is gonna be massive. I'm going to interview them tonight. You should take photographs of them and sell them when they've made it. I told you to bring your camera.'

John was a skinny bloke with freckles; an icky music journalist freak. Ten years earlier we'd been at Art College together. He used to paint band logos on leather biker jackets. He said he was going to be a latter day Lester Bangs. I said I was going to be a modern Nan Goldin. Now we were dangerously close to our thirties with no notable success. He worked for the local newspaper reporting magistrate cases. He did the record reviews for free. I, for all my flaws *was* a working freelance photographer. Wedding contracts, like dwarf sculptors wielding chisels, chipped fragments out of my soul, leaving patchy, disorderly holes in its surface. In the winter I lived on Drum tobacco and bacon flavoured Super Noodles.

Everyday was excruciating. Now and again we saw each other at rock concerts. We talked about the dreadful state of British music and the appalling effect capitalism was having on art. Most of all we talked about how well we were both doing; how much money we were pocketing, how close our big breaks were.

'Remember Eighties soft rock?' he said. 'People were happy when they were listening to men in lace-up spandex and codpieces. They liked Mötley Crüe. They didn't need some grungy smack addict telling them to load up on guns because life's not worth living. They know that. They want to have fun. They want entertainment. They want people like him,' he pointed at the singer, 'jumping all over the place. Smells Like Teen Spirit,' he said. 'People thought that song title was an iconic slice of genius. But it's not, Amb, it's bullshit. Teen Spirit is a brand of American deodorant, that song is nothing but a second rate limerick. I reckon that the world is ready for *this* band. I really do.'

'What're they called?' I said.

'The Dust!' he said. He grinned conceitedly, like he'd thought of the name himself.

I glanced around the room. The singer was standing on someone's shoulders, playing a solo in his black and white cat-suit stripes while the man beneath him walked through the crowd like he didn't have a thirty-five year old man on his back, playing a solo. The building collapsed into feedback and applause. The air was thick with the stench of sweat and charcoal. The small audience surged toward the stage wall like an army, their skin pink with energy and alcohol. The guitarist stepped down to light a cigarette and fifteen blue flames sparked up and shone, reflecting in his T-shirt's silver motif, like a Bon Jovi ballad. Everything about The Dust was delirious and I thought that for once John might just actually be right.

I followed him backstage where the little fat drummer was perspiring. The singer was holding a rolly in his palm, backwards, like a poor man with a lot to hide. It was the way woodwork teachers smoked on yard duty at my old comprehensive school. I didn't look away from his chunky belt buckle.

'I think you'll do well,' John said, reaching out to shake his hand.

'I think we will too,' the singer said. His voice was from eastern England. His fingers were small, his fingernails bitten.

'I'd like to interview you,' John said. 'If you have the time.'

'For what?'

'For being in The Dust. I want to interview the band.'

'Yeah,' the singer said. 'For which publication?'

'Oh, the *Observer*.'

'The *Observer*?'

'He means the *Pontypridd Observer*,' I said.

The singer raised his eyebrow theatrically and chuckled. 'Who are you?' he said.

'This is Amber, my photographer.' John put his arm around my shoulder and I shrugged it off.

'I'm a freelance photographer,' I said, staring so hard at his belt buckle I could feel myself beginning to squint. I moved down to the toes of his basketball boots. 'And I don't have my camera on me. What's your name?'

'It's Jason,' he said. 'Jason.'

We all smiled politely at one another, as though one of us wasn't wearing the most ridiculous item of clothing I'd ever encountered, and I didn't know what to say next. I couldn't do conversation sober. I decided to depart. 'I'll leave you to carry on with your interview,' I said. I was hoping to appear mysterious rather than aloof – I'd read in a book of quotations once that important people never stayed long. 'See ya.' When I found the door handle I turned out into the loud, claustrophobic bar, imagining Jason was watching me go, a gasp of perplexed marvel smacked over his kissy gob. I regretted it before the latch clicked back together and I sat on the edge of the empty stage, and bought eleven bottles of beer. I found the duplicate till receipts (the bane of the self employed) stuffed in my denim arse pockets much later.

Neither Jason nor John ever came back. I woke up outside, in the steel guttering beside the fire exit. A few yards away a big vehicle had left tyre trails in the frost. Invisible crows were squawking through the indigo dawn. And that, as they say, was that.

* * *

A week later my brain was addled with influenza. I laid in bed, bored, ill and horny. (It was probably some strange fantasy about nurses that I contracted unknowingly, having grown up with four brothers). I could hear the woman next door pegging washing on her rotary line as I masturbated. She was humming the tune to Nancy Sinatra's *These Boots Are Made For Walking*. I knew by the time lapses between the ticks of the pegs that she was hanging beach towels. My legs were stretched so wide across the mattress, I knew my hips would be stiff by the time I'd finished, and with that in mind, I popped; like toasted bread. The picture I was looking at when I climaxed was of a man with a thinning fringe, in a flamingo pink T-shirt, staring attentively at me, his brown eyes corroding my armour. It was starting.

I dressed. I tried to outrun my fever, jogging to the supermarket. When I got there my nostrils were dripping. I picked a mesh basket up out of the stack and shuffled into the artificial lighted store. Near the refrigerator I saw French hanging around the pasta aisle. French was my best school friend, an ugly girl who liked maths. Her child was hiding toffee apples in her trolley, under the nappies and toilet paper. I lifted my parka-hood over my head and searched for Welsh butter. It was hard to find Welsh butter. The supermarket was managed by people from Manchester. They only sold English products. Other things they did which is not typical Welsh behaviour included cutting the mould off the turned cheese and repackaging it as Cathedral City, defrosting chickens and advertising them as fresh, and emptying the RSPCA charity pet food box at night to reshelve the Whiskas. The security guard had told me these things as part of his chat-up lines.

'Amber? Is that you?' French was standing beside me, a box of lemon tea in her hand.

'Hiya French,' I said, my teeth clenched. 'I'm just looking for some butter.'

'I didn't know you still lived around here.' She was beaming. Was she implying that I was destined for a city because I was suave and creative, or did she imply that I was such a failure I had disappeared from her mind set. 'Look!' she said, thrusting the tea at me. 'I'm married, to Paul, from the chess club.'

'Oh,' I said dumbly.

'I'm taking India, my little girl to the surgery. I can't stop now. I'll give you my phone number – we'll have to go out.' She fumbled around in her leather handbag and scrawled a set of digits on a tissue paper.

'Yeah,' I said, slightly dismayed by the prospect, 'we will.'

It was dark early that afternoon. I baked a pie under the harsh light of the kitchen's bare bulb, the oven door wide open, the fan whirring. I lit each new cigarette with the one I'd just smoked, watching the grey pastry turn yellow. 'Listen you screw heads,' Joe Strummer said through the speaker in the living room next door, a script line from *Taxi Driver* superimposed into a Clash song, 'here is a man who wouldn't take it anymore.' Where is he? I thought. Where is Bobby DeNiro circa '76, beauty pocked and mohican-ed? Old. And fat. Where was Joe Strummer? Dead. All of my heroes were dead. I caught sight of my puffy eyes in the window pane. It was the onions that made me cry, I swear; sarcastic little fuckers. I turned the gas up to 8. Then I turned it down again in case the milk burned too quickly. Sylvia Plath said that pastry baking created some order in her otherwise chaotic life. Then one day, she baked her own head. Another girl dominated by the melancholic undercurrent that runs through life like a river; the hissing sound we're all trying to drown out. But they didn't make ovens like they used to.

I lifted the pie out and dusted the ginger crust away from the scooped edges of my grandmother's flan dish. The sweet odour of the crisp and golden flour caught at the back of my throat. I sneezed. The spittle landed in the centre of the pie. I wiped it away with the hemmed corner of the tea towel. The filling was cheap and fatty corned beef but to the rest of the world it could be steak and ale or mince and gravy. I'd discovered a cookery magazine that paid top whack for food shots. So long as the pastry looked edible they could say there were blackbirds inside. It didn't change a penny on my 2K cheque. I ran the tap for dishwater and swilled my grandmother's things, the marble rolling pin she beat my grandfather with and her wooden handle potato masher, thinking about the face of the flan dish where there was a finely painted pink rose, its head blooming, its arms still tight buds and its stem still green. Only I would ever know that it was there, like my La Bezella hand-embroidered lingerie.

I unpacked my camera and took some photographs.

* * *

Twelve hours later I was knocking on French's wooden front door. There was no bell, and no letterbox, just my bare knuckles rapping on a peeling layer of lilac paint.

At the other end of the street, in front of the Legion, a gang of kids were playing football with a stiletto shoe. The winter sun was going down behind them. Paul answered. He stood in the narrow passage with his hard, round belly standing out over his jogging bottoms, old tomato sauce stains around his sly mouth. He stared at the key-chain on my denim skirt. 'French here?' I said. I could hear my chewing gum and saliva swimming around in my words.

'Julia, you mean? Julia's here. She's not called French anymore,' he said. 'I married her.' He stood aside. I squeezed passed his naked skin.

'Cunt,' I said. The word hissed through the gap in my front teeth. I went into the first room I saw. French was sitting on the worn settee, lining her small, hollow eyes with a kohl pencil. 'You're here,' she said.

'Yep,' I said. I looked around the room, at the stacks of board games piled up on the fireplace. A white plate balanced on the arm of the chair, dirtied with Bolognese. Behind me her and Paul's daughter was swaying around the room, striking the furniture with a plastic wand.

'Do you want a glass of wine?' French said. I looked at the cheap table wine on the floor beside her winkle-pickers. Paul emerged from the porch, scratching himself. 'No thanks,' I said. 'We're late already.'

I threw my glob of chewing gum out of the car window and turned out of Elizabeth Street, onto the main road. French flicked her mousy curtains out of her face and pulled her shift dress down over her knees. 'I can't believe you married that wanker,' I said. I lit a cigarette.

'Amber!' she said. She leaned over to the window, away from me. 'He's India's father.'

'You mean you married him after you got pregnant?'

'No that's not what I mean,' she said. 'I married him four years ago yesterday.'

'Where was I?' I said. I dodged a crowd of teenagers running across the road into the disco at the old Banc, their hair thick with gluey substances, their bodies emitting Eau de Toilette like greenhouse gases.

'I don't know. I sent you an invite.'

'I don't like weddings,' I said. 'Marriage is for dicks.'

The car turned quiet. I turned the stereo on, flicked my cigarette butt out of the window and lit another. French was watching the towns drift passed. Through the wing mirror I could see that my comments hadn't wounded her. The corners of her mouth were turned up faintly. She was satisfied with herself.

'Where are we going?' she said as we approached the Royal Glamorgan Hospital. 'Did you say something about Def Leppard?'

'You still like Def Leppard don't you?' I said.

'Yeah.'

'Yeah?' I said. 'You fuckin' dork. You haven't changed at all. You're still the same old Frenchie. How can you like a band whose drummer only has one arm? I was so cool when I was sixteen, listening to *House of Pain* and *Sheep on Drugs*, and you were still on heavy metal! Ha!'

'You weren't cool,' she said. 'You were wild – just plain bloody nuts. And this was your idea.'

'You can watch Def Leppard if you want,' I said, 'but

I'm taking you to see the support band.'

'Why?' she said.

'Because,' I said, 'The Dust. I want to take some pictures of them. You'll like them.'

'The Dust?' she said, 'Is that a drugs reference?'

'No French,' I said, perturbed with her uselessness. 'It's a reference to depression. When you're depressed it's like your life is covered in dust and there's no polish to wipe it off.'

'Really?' she said.

Cardiff City opened up in front of us, the Millennium Stadium sitting in the middle of it like an enormous white beetle, the street lights flickering on, the office lights flickering off. Inside the International Arena we stood right in front of the stage. Jason did his stuff, his pink leather, his Lycra cat-suit, his guitar licks, his brown eyes, his cheekbones, his hair follicles. He didn't notice me. It happened a lot like that. First I noticed a man, then, when the opportunity to get to know him presented itself I ran away like a little girl from a stranger. I dreamt his personality up in my bedroom and went out searching for him again. He would have forgotten but I'd make him remember me. I could make him fall in love with me. I could make him want to marry me. I could break his heart. I could leave him and begin the game all over. It was a merry go-round that kept getting faster. It started with boys at school and meandered through novelists, footballers, other women's husbands. I thought that if it stopped, the world would stop. I'd only ever fallen off once, and Jason was my first fledgling rock star.

French watched the band, unsmiling, her eyeballs jumping out of her face like cartoon insects. She took plastic beakers of gin from me and swallowed them whole without moving anything but her forearm, even when I dropped a rock of Charlie in one. 'See French,' I said, my gums numb, my teeth stiff. The Def Leppard crowd were pushing us up against the steel barrier. 'They're good aren't they?'

She nodded at me, her mouth paralysed, her skin translucent.

'Are you coming backstage with me? I need to take some piccies.'

'No, I'm going to be sick,' she said.

'You're not,' I said. 'I have to do this, come on.'

'I don't feel well,' she said. 'I haven't drunk in years. I need to go back to the hotel, and you have to come with me, I don't know my way around Cardiff.'

'If we go back to the hotel you have to come to London with me tomorrow. They're playing in Brixton. I have to get the pictures. I promised John I'd get some pictures. Promise?'

'Yeah,' she said, and projectile vomited over the shoulder of a denim jacket in front of her. I saw the grains of cocaine amongst the bile, clinging to the hem and I vowed not to waste any more of it on her.

* * *

A day later we were in London. I parked my faithful green car in a Hammersmith multi-storey and took the underground to Brixton, the film cartons in my record bag butting one another on the steep escalator. French, like a lemming, followed. We drank warm Bavarian beer in a bar on the Town Hall Parade and tried not to look at one another too closely. I thought that if anyone would understand, French would. French knew me when I was a teenager so how could anything I did or felt in adulthood shock her? She'd know that rock music galvanised me, the same way it did all those years ago, when we still had school uniforms hung in our wardrobe and life was a glorious, endless opportunity waiting to be explored, and not just a lumpy, bumpy well trodden path; when nothing was gravely serious and it was still okay to fantasise about your fairy tale wedding to Johnny Depp. At first it had seemed like an adventure. She'd never been to London. But when we arrived she lost her appetite. The city's size and indifference had put her in a bad mood. She went to the toilet and I scratched at my two day old hipsters, the seams ripped on the insides of my thighs, my blood boiling as the second night of binge drinking kicked in.

'I'm on,' she whispered as she sat down, staring back at the flooded unisex cubicle as though its unseemliness had been the cause of her period. 'We have to go home, Amber. That's it, I knew this was a bad idea. Paul is gonna kill me.'

'What the fuck are you talking about?' I said. 'If Paul is India's father then he'll have no trouble looking after her for *one* day. Try to enjoy yourself. You promised me. And I promise you. We'll be home tomorrow.' I rifled through my bag and found a tampon, tobacco flakes clinging to its cellophane cover. I put it on the table and

French gawked at it. After a moment she clawed it and took it back to the loo. When she came back she was yawning. She sat at the table and rubbed her eyes with the balls of her hands, smearing mascara down her cheek. I didn't tell her. I popped the last green pill from my foil card and threw it on the table. 'I've had a drink now,' I said, 'but that was my last anti-depressant. We'll have to go home tomorrow.'

French grunted. I scanned the table flyers and considered moving to Brixton, knowing, even as I did that I couldn't afford to. It was only when the purple-mouthed waitress came to ask us if we wanted to order sandwiches that I noticed the only white girl in the building, other than me and French was Eliza Carthy, folk musician, daughter of Martin and girl about the big smoke, propping the bar, the *Evening Standard* in her lap.

'Excuse me, Eliza?' I said, resting my hand on the back of her high chair. Photography is fortuitous. It's like meeting the man of your dreams. Being competent helps but it's really all about presence, ending up at the right time, at the right place, with a camera in your bag. I used black and white film. She stared, dazed, at a poster on the other side of the room, her oriental eyes drowsy, the colourful cornrows in her hair falling loose. French watched, bemused, with the rest of punters as I snapped and wound. During a close up I noticed a preview for the gig at the Academy on Carthy's paper. The photograph wasn't of Def Leppard though; it was Jason with concealer on to hide his protruding bones and an ostrich feather in his hair. When I got back to the table French had eaten my cheese salad club sandwiches, the parsley garnish and all.

'C'mon, we have to go,' I said. 'We have to go get tickets.'

Outside the Academy, rain was pummelling out of the black sky. There was one tout in front of the building, a tall man in a brown mac.

'How much?' I said, raising my record bag over my head.

'Forty,' he said, 'each.'

'You're kidding,' I said. 'It's Def Leppard. They went legit for fifteen quid.'

'They went,' he said. 'Went is the operative word.'

'Have you got eighty quid on you?' I smiled at French.

She glared appallingly at me. 'I thought we had tickets,' she said. 'You made it sound like you had passes and everything.'

'I had passes for Cardiff, French. We had to leave, remember. You know what this means?'

'No way,' she said. 'We're going home tomorrow – you promised.'

'Unless you can lend me eighty squid we're going to be in Nottingham tomorrow.'

French ran away in the rain, swearing. I looked at the tout and he sniggered from behind his coat collar.

'French?' I screamed, turning down the street after her. 'French, come back. You don't know where you're going.'

*   *   *

The digital green numbers on my dashboard shone violently into the sombre darkness; 9.45 p.m.

'You'd only have ten minutes to get home now,' I said, 'if you were fifteen and you lived with your parents.'

French glowered at me from the passenger seat. Her long hair had congealed into thick ribbons under the heavy London rain.

'Are you sick?' she shrieked. 'I don't think your problem is depression, Amber. You're a psychopath. Kidnapping is illegal. That's what this is y'know. You told me we were going to see Def Leppard. Now we're in London. I haven't changed my clothes. I haven't been home for two days.' She pulled her shift dress down around her knees to cover a ladder in the thigh of her woollen tights.

'You'd always buy loads of junk food from Spar and sneak it up into your bedroom,' I said. 'Do you remember that? Bottles of Cola and pop-corn and cake bars. I thought you were bulimic.'

'Did you hear me?' she shouted.

'Keep your knickers on, French,' I said. 'Taking an old friend to a concert is not illegal. Drink driving is though. There are trains to Wales all night; you just get on the tube to Paddington. I'm not stopping you but I have to get to Nottingham now because you were sick in Cardiff.'

'I can't. You know I can't.'

'Why?'

'Money, I haven't got any.'

'There *are* cash machines in London.'

'I haven't got a bank account Amb, it's in Paul's name.' I looked at her and shook my head, mortified by her stupidity. 'Don't look at me like that,' she said. 'I wasn't sick on purpose. I wasn't sick of my own accord. You've been spiking me with dope or something, I know you have.'

I shook my head again and said nothing.

'I know you have,' she said. 'I've never felt like that before on my own.'

'I haven't,' I said.

'You did,' she said, 'and I want some more.'

'Maybe you are a psychopath,' I said.

'Maybe I am,' she said, 'and I'll kill you if I don't get anything to put me in a better mood.'

'Are you serious?' I said.

'Deadly.'

'Well there's a condition,' I said. I fumbled in my denim pockets for the money bag and the cling-film inside it. The coke was sitting on my palm like one of those mini voodoo dolls that make you itch. You know it's not something you should be messing about with, and definitely not something you should be getting the old school prefect into, but the temptation is just too much to bear.

'I know,' she said. 'I have to come to Nottingham. I will. But you have to get the photographs and then I have to go home. What's so special about the photographs anyway?'

I looked up from the powder which I was deliberately cutting with my own debit card and stared at her face. I wasn't sure if the question was derisive. Did she already know that it was about more than a picture?

'The band is going to be big. The photograph could be a spring-board.' I snorted first. 'Do it like this,' I said, 'snort, don't blow.'

'It's a funny life you live,' she said.

'It's better than marriage,' I said.

'It's not a disease,' she said, 'marriage. You crinkle your nose up like it smells bad.'

'It was the Charlie,' I said, coughing, 'but disease is a pretty good description.'

At four in the morning a security guard opened the wrought iron gates at the entrance to the multi storey. I started the engine and French sat up like a jack in a box, her pupils wide as dinner plates. She darted them around the car suspiciously and sat back. She plugged in her seatbelt, realising she was awake. She stretched her thick arms up into the air in front of her like an old cat. Then she folded them again and smoothed her upper arms with either hand, hugging herself. 'Cold,' she murmured.

I nodded, a wordless, sympathetic gesture. The road was slick from the storm and the tyres whipped against it, the sound of progression.

In a Burger King inside a service station just out of Bedford, she watched travelling salesmen pull up in estate cars and come inside to order coffee. I watched her as she wiped the mayonnaise out of her burger with her paper serviette.

'Always best to be careful,' I said.

'What?'

'I said it's always best to be careful. You must have heard the stories about the McDonald's in Llantrisant.'

'No,' she said.

'Closed them down. Girl got a few cold sores on her mouth after eating some chicken thing. She was a nurse from the Royal Glamorgan. She got it checked out and it tested positive for gonorrhoea. Some dirty bastard had been wanking in the mayo.' It was an urban myth that stretched the breadth of the United Kingdom but I guessed that French was gullible enough to buy it.

'Amber!' she said and she put her burger down on her tray.

'French?' I said, while she weighed the story up in her head, her hand resting protectively on her empty stomach. 'Have you ever fucked an Englishman?'

'No,' she said, peering around at the men in the room, hoping none of them heard my question. She didn't even have to think about the answer. 'Why?'

'I just wondered,' I said. 'It's sacrilegious isn't it? We're from the Welsh valleys. It's like an Irish Catholic shagging a British soldier. It's punishable with tar and feathers. I just wondered if you'd ever committed that sin.'

'Have you?'

'Not yet,' I said and she smiled at me. 'Something else,' I said. 'If you meet someone you like on Valentine's Day, is that fate? Is a meagre coincidence like that meaningful?'

'Do you want me to answer that?' she said, 'Or is it a joke?' I was looking ahead at the queue for the counter. 'If you want it to be, I suppose,' she said and she shrugged her shoulders. 'But you said it was a meagre coincidence. So probably not.'

'Mmm,' I said. That's all I said, but she was right. It was probably not fate or destiny or anything mysterious pushing me toward Jason from The Dust. It was just me having one of my silly obsessions, me looking for things to make my life more interesting. I wondered what would happen if I stopped chasing rainbows. I wondered if I'd die, like other depressed people, or if I'd find something meaningful to do. Maybe I was the one with a disease. 'Are you happy with Paul?' I said. 'Is he really all that?'

French was picking the sesame seeds from the top of her bun with her fingernail and balancing them on her tongue until the urge to bite them became a necessity.

'You stole all the others,' she said. She was silent for a few seconds while she let her sentence impact on me. 'Paul was the only one who didn't want you. He was the only one who wanted me. So you see, he'll have to do.'

Backstage at Rock City that night, I tilted my head back and threw a glass of warm red wine into my mouth. French's small eyes, outlined in smoky and smudged eye-shadow she'd managed to smuggle on in the wing mirror, danced around the room. My head swam, my legs were splayed out on a glass coffee table, my camera case in my lap. Every few minutes I tried to sit up straighter, the leather underneath me making farting sounds, my dye-damaged curls falling into my face. The anxiousness in my bones pounded harder, making its presence felt above the alcohol. I was nervous because I was going to meet him and tired because I hadn't taken my medication.

'There he is,' French said.

I sprung up, knocking a paper plate of tiger prawns from the arm of the Chesterfield. The floor felt like a rubber dinghy on a lake as I ran towards him, through a throng of smoking journalists with all access passes pinned to their nipples. I followed rock's young dream as it stumbled down a dark corridor in jeans it had sprayed on, a rip in the arse of them stuck down with electrical tape, a bottle of Smirnoff in its hand.

'Jason?' I said.

He pirouetted to face me. 'I know your name,' he said. 'I do. What's your name?'

'Amber.' Amber. It's the colour of the traffic light that tells you to get ready, either to stop or go. And that's where I'm stuck, forever getting ready.

'Amber,' he said. 'You following me or what?'

'I've got my camera,' I said.

'Okay, whatever,' he said. In the doorway to his dressing room he gave me the bottle of vodka and I sat on a wooden chair. He got naked with his back to me while I glugged on the neat spirit, holding my hand over my closed mouth while I swallowed, so nothing dribbled out. When he wasn't naked anymore I took two pictures of him in his ripped T-shirt, leaning against the stained sink. I was too scared to get close enough to do a light reading in case I lurched at him, so I used a flash which was too strong. His brown eyes disappeared to pin-pricks in the back of his skull.

'Do I know you from somewhere else?' he said. 'I think I already recognised you the first time.'

'No, I don't think so,' I said, I took four more pictures

while he spoke. When I stopped and put the camera away, he stopped talking and I had no witty comment to snare him like a fish hook. 'Well that's it,' I said, 'thanks.'

'You've got your pictures,' he said.

'Yes,' I said and I began to feel for the door handle behind me.

'And now you're leaving me all alone?'

'What makes you think I wouldn't?'

'I know what lust smells like,' he said.

'I think it's your vodka, actually,' I said. 'People say it has no odour, but it does. It's a wheaty, grubby smell. That's how groupies smell. I'm just a photographer.' I found the door handle. 'I'll see you later,' I said. 'I'm going.' I did glance back at his cow-brown irises but his eyelids were firmly closed.

* * *

'You can't drive, Amb,' French said. 'You've been drinking.'

'Yeah, but we have to get home.'

'I'll drive,' she said.

'You can't drive,' I said.

'I can,' she said. 'Paul taught me.'

'Are you sure?' I said.

'Would I lie about that?' she said. 'Would I lie about anything?'

'Well, quickly then; we have to go before I want to go back in.' I got into the passenger seat and found my mobile phone in my record bag. I switched it on.

'Is that a phone?' she said. 'Did you have a phone all

along? You're a fucking bitch, Amber. I could have phoned him.'

'You never asked,' I said. 'You never told me you could drive, you could have driven home from London instead of giving me shit about kidnapping you. *You're* a fucking bitch.'

I tried to ring John. I wanted to tell him I had a picture, that I finally had the picture, that all I had was a picture, but there was no answer. 'I'm going to get a dog,' I said, throwing the phone back into my bag.

'Why?' she said.

'Well first you get a plant and if that doesn't die you get a dog. If that doesn't die you have a kid.'

'Well then you need a plant first.'

'I've got one, a cactus.'

'But before you get a kid you need a husband.'

'I could buy a kid,' I said, 'from Russia.'

A Little Boy

The mattress underneath her was cold with sweat. She dare not move. She just lay there, crunching her pelvic floor into a painful crease to save pissing on the sheet, knowing, even in the dark, that it was going to be a malicious day. It was written in the way the pretty embroidered blue flowers on the drawn voile curtains hung their heads, trounced by the frost on the pane. Next to her, Dan breathed heavily as though a dream was trying to throttle him. She wondered how she sounded *when* she slept, if she screamed, or dozed calmly, knowing all too well that life was one long nightmare that you could never wake out of. Then he opened his eyes quite abruptly, as though he'd felt her gaze on his body.

'I love you,' he murmured, reaching for her with his slow arms. She rolled away from him, landing a swollen foot on the cold, bare floorboard, and she sidled laboriously out of bed. She despised him saying that because he said it unconsciously, too often, like it was an Anadin capsule that could make everything okay again. But she was never going to be okay. It was what Godfrey used to say before he lifted her school shift dress, and she was suspicious that it was some sort of secret code men used, not to express fondness, but supremacy.

She stood at the wash basin in the kitchen, carelessly swilling mugs. Outside, winter had robbed the trees of their foliage, and their twisting branches seemed to grasp rather than dance. The pine trees on the Rhigos Mountain stood with their shoulders pinched as though trying to avoid the dew that fell on them, because when it hit it turned instantly to ice. The sky was red. A tom cat cried at the bottom of the garden but its desperation was unrequited. Mog, her own tabby cat had disappeared two months ago. She wasn't sure if Mog was jealous of her or disgusted by her, and after a week she'd washed and put away the clay dishes and the squeaky mice, her eyes fuzzy with tears. Slowly, the pictures she'd seen in the night came back to her mind's eye, winding and throwing her heaving into the sink below her. At one point she was sure she'd seen a thickset blonde man pull a quilt back on the bed to reveal the small boy underneath it. The bed was a double so he looked extra little, nestled between the pillows. The bed clothes were white, so his fair hair looked finer, almost invisible, and the blood looked more black than red. It swam over his stomach and his damp chicken thighs, like melting dark chocolate, in some areas glutinous and others congealed, so she couldn't actually work out whether his anus had been bleeding, or his baby penis had been cut. And she wasn't sure if he was sleeping, or if he was dead, if that volume of blood loss could kill a boy that age. She wasn't sure now if it was a premonition or if the pictures had only been a dream, some sort of fake snuff show her own mind had created to frighten itself stiff.

She turned the key in the back door and the rime in the air punched at her naked calves. She quickly lit her cigarette, protecting the hiss from the flame of the lighter with her curled hand, a practised and essential procedure if she was to conceal it from Dan, two floors away. As she stood smoking in the murk of the dawn, the little boy kicked at the banister, as though to confirm her night visions *had* been real. She turned resignedly to look at him, pouting on the stairs, his lamb-print dungarees too colourful for the situation, and saw his beseeching puppy eyes, plain as the day. She shook her head helplessly and sighed her fetid smoke out into the ether. She was happy to bolt the door closed again, swallowing her tobacco cough, as she heard Dan's severe footsteps on the stairs. He had smaller feet than her but he used them like warnings. It was a trait he'd acquired at birth from her father-in-law. The Hughes men used their bodies to make as much noise as a body possibly could. They bellowed when they spoke, stamped when they walked, snored and ground their teeth. To a taciturn girl it was all quite upsetting and she prayed that her child would follow her, rather than him. She believed that silence, as a manner, *was* golden, it allowed her to listen, and therefore see. But what she saw was beginning to hurt her.

The noise scared the boy too and he lifted his big head out of his hands and stared up into the gloomy living room, like a cornered rat, forgetting himself and all of his immediate escape routes. Dan passed him on the stairs without a flinch or a sniffle, his black cotton boxers fading grey and turning soft. His hard thighs were dotted with fine brown hairs but towards his shins his skin became white, and bald.

'Cold out there, looks like,' he said, and she saw the boy peer at her from between Dan's knees, his face trying to press something urgent into her head, in the way other kids at the supermarkets pleaded for sweets, before he crawled the treads with his four limbs, like a monkey, and vanished at the top.

'Probably is,' she said, stirring the milk into their coffee. It spiralled in so the liquid turned seamlessly from black to white, its tart smell piping up into the back of her throat. She closed her nostrils quickly so she did not vomit.

When she passed it to him, he leaned to kiss her and she swooped away like a magpie, hardly hiding her repulsion, partly because she didn't want Dan to taste the smoke, still lingering in her mouth but mostly because the thought of physical, sexual contact made her more queasy than the saccharine aroma of instant coffee. They hadn't touched, not even their fingertips, for months on end. She had finished work one month before and as she stared at the television screen, thinking about what the people at her office were doing, she sometimes found herself drifting off into dirty daydreams, but the man beside her, pleasuring

138

her was anyone but Dan. She thought she was ugly as a baboon, plodding around in beige maternity clothes with something other than her own organs growing inside her, like a presumptuous tumour.

Sometimes when she halved a yellow pepper there'd be another smaller one inside and she recoiled in horror. Dan had made her that way, with his seed, which made him unattractive too, and the more he told her how blooming and peachy and beautiful she looked the more she began to suspect foul-play. He wanted her out of work, out of sight, her belly full of his babies. She should never have agreed to it, the world was a gruesome place which bullied its population for fun. There were too many people in it already and it was about to blow up, so why should she plague it with her own spawn? She was a prime candidate for post-natal depression too.

Dan pretended not to notice her dread and cordially smiled his way out of the front door and on to work, miles away, his safety boots clunking to the kerb.

The day didn't bring any light so she sat on the bed in what was going to be the nursery, hoping for the first hour that the boy would return and finally speak. The moment passed. He never came when she was fully awake, and he never came to the bedroom. Then, as she drifted into a now familiar kind of inert limbo, the man's face that drifted through her head's internal projection struck her enough to shake herself conscious. She'd seen Eric, her auntie's boyfriend, twenty years younger than he was now, sitting skinny and naked chested with a cine camera in his lap, his hair long and scraggy. In the background, a small boy had been crying. She thought about Eric. She'd never liked him; in fact she disliked him a lot. When her uncle died of cancer a year or two ago her aunt had found a new lease of life and she began placing personal ads in the local newspapers, and wearing nail polish on her toes, and drinking alcopops, like a merry teenage widow. She'd never shared a bed with her husband, or so much as glanced at a skirt that landed above the knee in Marks & Spencer's. The result of all this nonsense was Eric, who'd moved in within a week, saying he was a Canadian best selling sci-fi author called Wilton Devonelle. But he spoke with a cockney accent and he was thick as big-dog shit.

When she met him it had been sunny and he was sitting in her uncle's string hammock playing with the duck eggs. He'd taken them from under Bessy, a few hours before they were due to hatch and he was peeling the blue shell, like an orange. Half way down he'd stab the papery skin underneath with a long, brittle fingernail and show her the duckling inside, a pink and red creature, the size of a thumb, coated in slippery mucus. She wasn't sure if he could kill a duck like that, but either way, he didn't seem to care. He casually placed the broken shell on the grass beside him, ignoring Bessy's relentless hiss, and started on the next. She looked at his face and could see from the way his mouth turned upward that he took pleasure from it; he liked spoiling things. He was grainy too, like he'd forgotten to wash the grout out of his nicotine wrinkles. And she immediately began to think him unctuous, and creepy. His eyes were the same ones Godfrey used to look at her, careless and lawless and hungry. The air between them turned like a screw, gathering pressure by the second, and she shivered, and left.

At home she found black and white photographs of Wilton Devonelle on the internet, a big, perm-haired man with content bovine eyes and a handle-bar moustache. She tried to tell her auntie but her auntie said that Eric had an interesting life and had probably changed a lot over the years, and anyway, hadn't she heard of a pen-name? She'd never found the courage to go back. The entire stomach-turning scenario went through her like reptiles; she could almost feel their scales scuffing against the walls of her veins, itching, whenever she thought about her auntie, or about science fiction. Eric was a sad fantasist, so disappointed with his own life he had to make a new one up, and how much that had to do with the possibility of him once being involved in a ring of paedophilia, she was now timorously, frenziedly, evaluating.

'I've got something to tell you,' she said, speaking slowly and guardedly to the police officer who had sounded quite genial when he answered, *Hello, Ton Pentre Police Station*, he'd said, in a musical tone. She'd imagined him smiling with the crumbs and the jam from his biscuits still clinging to the wedges in his teeth. 'It's about child abuse,' she said, thrusting her finger through the curled navy wire attaching the receiver to the telephone.

'Before you go on,' he said, becoming as cagey now as she was, 'are you sure you want us, or do you want the social services? Is there a child at risk?'

'No,' she said, and she was silent for a moment wondering what was at risk. It was her sanity, surely. 'It's a bit strange actually. It's about a recurrent dream I have, and a ghost.' She heard the policeman suck air over his teeth. The whistle on the connection pierced. Even she thought the idea of psychics trying to solve murder cases was daft and she sympathised with him. 'I won't tell you the details, you won't believe them. I just want you to check something for me.'

'Be quick then love,' he said, 'I'm busy.' Suddenly he sounded busy.

'I'm suspicious about somebody who lives on the Swyn-yr-Afon estate,' she said. 'He's staying with my auntie. I don't know his full name, only Eric, he's called Eric. You have sex offender registers at your fingertips and maybe he's on one. I just want you to remember him, so if something happens. If something –'

'That's it?' he said. 'That's all you know?'

'Yes.'

'Well there isn't much I can do.'

'I know, but maybe in the future you'll need to know who he is. Maybe if a small boy went missing, or something untoward went on near the estate, maybe the person you'd be looking for would be Eric. It's number ten.'

'Are you joking?' he said. 'Because we take child abuse very seriously. We take you accusing somebody of child abuse very seriously.'

'I'm not joking. I'm not accusing him either, not really, and I take child abuse very seriously,' she said. 'Very seriously,' she said again.

'Okay, if that's all you wanted, I'll try to keep it in mind.'

'Thank you,' she said and she replaced the handset, feeling crushed. She stared out into the street where rain fell like an army of needles, penetrating the cracks in the pavement, and she found herself smoothing her hand over her hard, swollen belly, like somebody who was proud. She shrugged her shoulders. At least the policeman would have something to smirk over at the bar of the Prince of Wales that night, or maybe he would think about Eric. Perhaps he'd lie awake all night thinking about Eric.

But she slept. Only once did she peel her eyes open in panic as she felt something touch her hand. At a restaurant a few months ago, when she still thought herself appealing enough to be seen in public, a woman on the table behind Dan had been talking about horror films, and how the last one she'd seen had scared her out of dropping her arms at the side of the mattress. The woman's shrill voice was so aghast that she too had begun to keep her arms under the duvet, even though she'd never heard of the film title. Now she expected to see the boy, clutching onto her fore or middle finger like a newborn would. People thought that was exquisite, but she found the difference in scale alarming. She was beginning to shrink into herself, her flesh tightening on her bones, when she realised that what she felt was fur. It was Mog, thinner, her eyes glistening prettily, hankering for jellied rabbit and liver. Through the voile she saw a glow in the black sky, something moving, like a firework, or a meteor storm, or the moon, but she was too tired to investigate. She closed her eyes, rolling gracelessly on her padded body, and she snored rhythmically with Dan next to her, like they were the church bells of neighbouring villages, answering one another at a distance.

Dan woke her up after his alarm had bleeped and he'd showered, water dripping from his body and staining the ink on the envelope in his hand.

'What's this?' she said, confused by him, and his gift and the numbers on the digital clock, her hair curling like a 1920's demi-wave, where her head had wedged into the pillow for a full nine night-time hours.

'It's Valentine's Day,' he said, smoothing his damp palm on her forehead. Her instinct was to lunge away from his contact but there was nowhere to go. Surprisingly, his fingers were soft and light and while he continued to pet her she actually felt lovely, required and lovely. She ripped the paper of the watermarked envelope with numb fingertips, Dan smiling at her ungainliness, growing eager as she did.

That morning the boy was nowhere to be seen or sensed. Strange smells, like milk and flowers and shit did not burst to life under her nostrils on the staircases. The temperature never wavered. It was just plain winter. She stood at the sink watching a ray of wild sunshine try to slice through the silver lining of a cloud. Upstairs Dan was whistling. She'd been awake for a full fifteen minutes before Godfrey entered into her thoughts. He came like an embarrassing memory rather than a wrecking ball. For a moment the skin of her face burned but the sensation crumbled away with her indifference, and her firm cheeks sprung white again. Unexpectedly, it seemed so simple – Godfrey was a miserable old man who'd stared at and touched the private pink places of her body that only her and her mother knew existed. He did it because he was weak, because his mind was warped. It wasn't right of course, but it wasn't her defect. She was caring and careful and good, and alive, and loved.

Come to think of it, she was everything a mother should be. She shook the washing up bubbles from her hands and a cluster landed on her protruding belly. The baby moved inside her, as though it had felt it, like a teenage girl caught by the watering hose of her brother during her sunbathing. She knew now why she'd carried the baby full term. It was because she wanted to give it a childhood of innocence, of games and happiness and protection. It was because she wanted it.

Jigsaws

It was 1977 and the sun was throbbing on the Rhondda. My mother pushed me around the market, the Gingham-cloth sun-umbrella on the pushchair crashing into stall pegs and other prams. It was okay then to leave a baby alone for a minute. I could hear her laugh in the distance; a wicked, fun-loving cackle. But I was strapped into my seat staring fixed at the goods, a pair of red tartan trousers with a high waist and wide legs pinned to a tarpaulin, a huge, smooth pomegranate going yellow in the weather. Then she'd take me to my cousin in the café where the steam from the coffee machine made the glasses on the shelf behind it wobble.

'Here's my other baby,' Mrs Carpanini would say. Her voice drew her big family from the back rooms into the shop where they'd smile and gurgle at me, all olive skin and jet black hair. 'Quick, quick,' she'd say, clapping her hands at Julia, my cousin. 'Get a drink for Heidi.' I remember the smell, tobacco from the old men's strong cigarettes and cocoa butter, the lotion on my skin, the sour taste of lime or cherryade, its gas at the back of my throat. I'd sit on a green leather bench next to the window, looking out through the multicolour vinyl blinds, my legs swinging beneath me, Paolo the Carpanini baby holding my hand, his orangey skin sweaty. Our mothers sat opposite us, talking about us, mine slipping neat forkfuls of steamed beef pie into her mouth between words, Mrs Carpanini playing with the skin under her chin. Always in the background there was the sound of clanking crockery, Julia replacing the cups and saucers they'd used that morning, an apron tied round her waist, a biro balancing behind her ear, nuzzling into her sandy colour curls.

'You mustn't tell Mammy about this,' Julia would say, spooning hazelnut chocolate into my mouth, the plastic spoon tapping on my milk teeth. My mother would have gone to work letting me sleep in the cool, shady back room of the café. But I'd cry for sweets, the room next door was full of them, screw top jars full of gelatine and sugar.

'Give her the Nutella,' Mrs Carpanini would say. 'We can't sell chocolate in this heat. She loves the Nutella.' Paolo would sleep opposite me on a wooden frame settee, pillows all around him so he didn't roll onto the floor. When he woke he'd walk over to me and lightly press his hand on my head. '*Ti amo*,' he'd say, looking down at me with enormous blue eyes. He could talk better than me. '*Ti amo*.'

I didn't know what it meant but I started saying it myself, at nursery and at home.

'I think it's time you were in bed, Heidi,' my father would say.

'*Ti amo*,' I'd say.

'What's she saying?' he'd say to my mother. 'She's talking Italian? Jesus, she can't speak Welsh yet!'

At the end of the afternoon Julia took me home. She took me across the road to see the Moscow State Circus at the Parc and Dare once. I've never forgotten it. There was a part where a man boxed with a kangaroo but nobody believed me when I told them. I told Marc a year or so ago and he said my memory had failed me, nobody would ever be allowed to fight with an animal – it must have been inflatable. But it was the Seventies; I remember the colour of its hair, not fluffy like a rabbit but wiry like a cat, and silver. I remember its red boxing gloves. I swear to this day it was a real kangaroo.

I grew up anyway, to be twelve or thirteen and kangaroos didn't interest me anymore, very little did; the pop band Wham! or maybe a strappy pair of shoes I couldn't walk in, maybe a boy now and again. Paolo grew to be tall and thin with a big round head covered in chocolate colour hair. At comprehensive school he surpassed me academically, got sent to A classes for science, maths and languages. He was the same inside as he was when he ran around his café in a nappy, benevolent and peaceful. He sent me Christmas cards years after I stopped. His tie was always neat. I felt sorry for him I suppose, thirteen year old boys were gruesome things with pockets full of stones, mouths full of swear words; it seemed wrong that he should still be so tender. It was a Friday morning when he touched me; rain pissing down on the annexe roof. I put my hand on the door handle to check if the classroom was locked; the teacher was five minutes late. He put his hand on top of mine, just for a second but I noticed the variation in our skin colours. We played with a general knowledge board game for the next hour under the eyes of a supervision teacher. Paolo won. My skin felt strange all day, tingly, and I wondered if he'd made a mistake or if he'd meant to do it, calculated it so I'd think about him all weekend.

A week later I was getting ready to go to Mrs Carpanini's birthday party. She'd invited me through Paolo. '*Il nostro bambino sta diventando grande*, Dominic!' she'd say to her husband. 'Our baby's getting big.' I'd imagined it all. Then my father called me down the stairs.

'You're not going,' he said. 'I don't want you going near that café. They're not like us, sweetheart. They're Italian, they're Catholic, they're different to us.'

'Daddy?!' I said. I wanted to say other things too but I was too shocked to find the words.

'What?' he said. 'What do you want, Heidi? You're growing up now, getting older. Do you want to be a designer or do you want to work in a café dropping babies after Italian babies? Now forget it, you're not going.'

In 1995 I married Marc, the son of my father's best friend, a big sinewy man who built houses for a living. Our fathers insisted we choose *Cwm Rhondda* as one of the hymns, that the reception be held in the rugby club and ceremony in the Non-conformist chapel. They organised all of these things for us. By the time the wedding came around it seemed as though Marc and me were only there to make up the numbers, a couple of eighteen year old kids still unsure of their own minds, guided carefully through the most important aspects of their lives by wise and virtuous parents. Marc didn't have an opinion about anything; deep down I thought that was his most attractive feature. My father bought a plot of land in the next village, an uneven surface winding up into the mountain and told Marc to build a house on it, a stout, white bungalow two miles away from the market, the café and my mother. I spent the first year of my marriage with a *Media Guardian* in my hand, picking out graphic designer appointments and circling them in red ink. Sometimes, I got as far as folding an application letter into an envelope, I don't think I ever posted one; the post office was so far away. I painted every wall inside the house magnolia with a small brush I found on the roadside. Marc never decided on a colour and the plaster got to boring me. I got up at five in the morning to fry bacon for sandwiches. By September I'd consummated the task so the bacon was thick and pink in the middle, brown and crisp at the edge.

The sky was grey on my first wedding anniversary. The wind shook the daisies on the hill back and forth, their heads nodding at some warning sent from the atmosphere. Marc was in Pembrokeshire building luxury apartments for professional couples. I walked down town to see my mother, cold biting at my ankles, nature dragging blood and lining from my womb. Near Dominic's a pang hit me between my ribs, maybe a hunger pain, a period pain, I didn't know. I slowed down at the window and looked at the Turkish Delights in their jar; caster sugar gathered an inch thick at the base. It was Dominic's now, plain and informal. No 'the café,' no connotations.

If I said, 'the café', Marc would say 'which café?'

'The Italian café.'

'There's five bloody Italian cafés down there.'

Julia wasn't there anymore. She didn't marry but she had children and she took them to the city. Paolo was serving and it relaxed me. Mrs Carpanini wasn't there to say, 'Oh my bambino!' I was a woman now. I watched him weigh out the wine gums, the mini eggs, reach for the Nutella sachets at the bottom of a jar until it was a mountain of colourful confectionary mounting on the peeling counter before me.

'My sweet tooth's playing up,' I said suddenly, defending my gluttony.

Paolo looked at me, his eyes still huge and cold like an ocean in winter, but he laughed warmly. '*Ti amo,*' he said quietly so the old men didn't hear. '*Ti amo.*' I looked away quickly to the clumsy old till and watched the numbers appear as he rang in the sale. Outside it was cold again and I realised that for a long time I had missed the sound of saucers clink.

Weary, I decided to set up a business, nothing big or fancy, just an Apple Mac in the spare bedroom to print wedding and Christening invitations. My father laughed at me.

'You're not a school child any more,' he said. 'You're a kept woman. Go dress shopping in Cardiff, or have a baby.' The business didn't get to trading anyway. I had a black eye on the day of my meeting at the bank. It turned out Marc did have opinions. He didn't like me lying in bed with a hot water bottle balancing on my midriff – he liked dinner on the table when he arrived. For a successful man, he had quite a lot to prove.

The café was dark that year. When I passed, it looked sad and heavy. An ice cream advert in the window fell down and crumpled on the sill. Nobody picked it up or blu-tacked it back to the glass. Paolo wasn't there; I thought perhaps he went to university, or travelling through Europe. At Easter Mrs Carpanini's newborn baby girl died of cot death. She had a massive funeral and the shop was closed for three weeks. When I did go in to buy cigarettes, nobody noticed me. The family were grieving for their real flesh. Then, my own father died. A lifetime of business deals and whiskey drinking ended. He was young to die but I wasn't sorry. I'd come to dislike him for his manipulation and contradictions. I'd tolerated him because he was my father but I'd realised how bitter and selfish he was, unhappy unless he had something to complain about; even my mother said she was relieved, he'd killed himself with his own aggravations. At the grave side Marc and his father wept more than we did.

A week later I filed for divorce. It was ugly but it was necessary, like a cervical smear. We'd both wasted two years of our young lives and now we felt old, used, depreciated. Marc didn't want a house that he'd built for his ungrateful ex-wife so he gave it to me; the land was my mother's now anyway. I washed him out of there, painting the walls terracotta and sunshine yellow, lilac and ocean blue. I threw the frying pan in the bin. I left my wedding and engagement rings in a vase on my father's grave.

The following Christmas I moved my boyfriend Kelis into the house. He was a student of architecture, four years younger than me, a boy with milk white skin, a washboard torso and half a dozen moles making the shape of a triangle across his belly, an indifferent face with cruel, black eyes, hair that stuck in place if you ran your fingers through it, ninety-eight pence in the bank, enthusiasm by the bucket load. It was enchanting at first like most new things. We don't stop playing with toys just because we grow up; the toys get bigger too. The house was full of wine, marijuana and the scents of expensive perfume. I ordered food from the delicatessen's, stone-baked pizzas with Parma ham and rocket salads and stopped washing dishes. I left clothing and possessions where they first got strewn so the sight of a diamante encrusted high heel shoe balancing on a stair, or a pair of joke shop handcuffs hanging from the bed frame excited me on uneventful Monday mornings.

I got a job as a librarian and dressed for sex in lace hold-ups hidden neatly under my uniform. It looked as though I was hard at work in the reference section cataloguing the local census but in my head I was draped across the machines in my utility room, my legs assuming an impossible position in the air. Sex was everything. It was the reason Kelis and me were together, the reason he was there. It was what everything else lead to – a final act everyday. We drank for sex, ridiculous percentages of alcohol printed in italics on the foot of bottle labels, all to loosen our restrains, to help us utter filthy words into one another's ear canals. We went to rock clubs to watch men play guitars, to shake off our day jobs, to smell sweat in the air, and go home to have sex, to fuck, skin never tasted so good and I wondered if Marc discovered it too, the animal instinct that comes with wanting someone, not for life but just for a night, or a week or a month, just until your energy has run out. Probably he didn't, he wanted to own everything. Of course, after the sex there wasn't much left, company on a cold night and a record collection full of aggressive, adrenaline-pumping guitar chords. I'd graze myself on the great big art folder Kelis carried around and on arrival left next to the front door. Before I'd look at it fondly and think it was cute; naive but powerful in its naivety. Now I swore at it or kicked it or hid it away in the louvre door cupboard. I let him stay though there was no bond between us, just a few more cupfuls of semen. I took keep when I could for food and water, pretended to be five years younger when his mother phoned and we carried on as a quasi-couple, sleeping in one bed and kissing now and then but all the while holding out for something better.

It was raining on the day it ended. Sheets of dirty water shot to the floor, droplets like bullets hitting and stinging pink skins, wind blowing umbrellas inside and out again. Kelis came to the library for me, his folder held with white knuckles, his little black eyes darting in panic for himself and disregard for me. He was going to see his friend's band he said, in Pontypridd, and he was late. I knew he had a date and I wasn't jealous. We used to walk to the bungalow, laughing. In the summer he'd take his sweatshirt off and tie it around his small waist. In the autumn we'd kick through the leaves, but we waited for a bus that day, standing in the freeze outside Dominic's, Kelis watching the square anxiously for the bustler to roll in and me turned to the window looking at how the colours of the blinds had faded in the sun to a beige, the red and green barely visible. I could see the gas fire on inside but that's not what made the shop front glow. The wood had rotted to a dull white, the wallpaper looked dated. The florescent strip light shone yellow against the night.

'Let's go in,' I said.

'What?' he said.

'Let's go in,' I said. I opened the door, pushing the brass rail handle away from me.

'Heidi,' Kelis said, 'the bus will be here any minute.'

'The bus is always late,' I said. He didn't push the matter any further; he didn't want to protest too much. It was there, stirring my cappuccino and relishing the sound of the spoon against the china that I realised it's always the same, all over the world: boy meets girl, boy meets another girl, girl meets boy, girl meets another boy. It's a jigsaw and sometimes the pieces don't fit. What do you do? You try another piece. You keep trying until it's complete or your jigsaw looks shitty. The cups were the same as before, white with a burgundy band around the rim. When I looked at the glasses on the shelves closely they still wobbled behind the steam from the percolator.

'Drink your coffee,' Kelis said, but I was trying not to hear him.

Paolo had walked through from the back room. He was standing behind the counter staring at me, the ribbons hanging from the door still draped over his shoulders. Sometimes the jigsaw piece was right first time; it was other things that needed to fall into place.

'Drink your coffee,' Kelis said. 'The bus is here.'

'Go then,' I said, 'get on the bus. I haven't finished *my* coffee.'

Twenty-six years old and I was still a kid in a sweet shop.

The Brake Fluid at Gina's

'Are you gonna eat somefin' today, baby doll?'

Ruth was sitting on the forecourt, the sharp plastic mouldings of an orange box pressing into the seat of her overall. She couldn't see Gina tapping the base of her biro against the empty page in the diary. She yelled back at the English voice in the dark workshop. 'No, I'm okay boss, honest.' She slurped from the warm, red can of soda beside her feet.

It was Sunday, and August – too quiet to walk to town. On the summer weekends there were rock bands on the bandstand in Ynysangharad Park. She'd seen groups of kids dawdling across the roundabout in their drainpipe jeans and *Guns 'n' Roses* T-shirts, the girls in hot pants and boob tubes. Their plastic grocery bags weakened around the weight of their cider. Kids from the valley were around.

It was perilous to run to Wimpy for a carton of fries, or to the pub for takeaway faggots for Gina. She sat under the sunshine of her permanent cigarette break, imagining life on the other side of the park fence; leisurely hours of grass blades tickling bare elbows and the scent of deodorant fading away. At the garage there was only concrete, ceaselessly stained with the pungent whinge of oil.

Otherwise, Pontypridd was a clever place to hide. When she'd arrived eighteen months earlier, it was February. She'd stood on the enormous railway platform, waiting for a connection while daylight drenched the mountains. The flaps and squawks of pigeons quarrelling over the flaky breakfast pastry echoed under the fibre glass shelters. It was a lonely Victorian wasteland where miners from the three adjoining valleys congregated at the height of the industrial age for union meetings and rugby matches, and mile-long strings of cars filled with coal pummelled over the tracks. That morning she stood stiff enough to feel the dusty, phantom crowds shadowing around her and figured one more ghost wouldn't make any real difference. In the weekdays the dirty streets stirred with students and office workers and market traders and tramps. People danced in a fierce festival of living. She'd see old neighbours from the valley on giro days, their trolleys heavy with frozen meats, but they'd never see her. On Wednesdays she could buy the old district newspaper to look at which one of her brothers won the trials race at the motor club on the previous Saturday. It was a torturous comfort that reminded her they still worked under the same rain clouds. One time she saw Nathan's initials scratched with a pen knife into the underside of a mudguard. Fifteen miles – it was like the length of a piece of string.

Gina wheeled her office chair out onto the fudgy forecourt and sat down next to Ruth. She rolled a liquorice tobacco paper between her fingernails, suspiciously watching families drive away from the garden centre.

'Rufe, doll, you sure you ain't got nothin' better to do on a Sunday? Huh? Than hang around here wiv an old lesbian like me?' Ruth smiled sorrowfully and shook her head. Gina lit her DIY cigarette with her petrol Zippo. She sucked it as she narrowed her eyes to the sky. The skin was soft and creased around her eyelids and her kohl bled into the gaps, like insect legs. When she started work at the garage, Ruth tried to imagine Gina in bed, with her thick neck and sausage thumbs. She thought about how ridiculous her hard words would sound against a soft pillow. Now it was tough to think of her as anything other than maternal. 'There are no bookings,' she said. 'We're sitting here waiting for nuffing.' Ruth smoothed her hair out of her face and retied her ponytail-band. Gina nudged her so she shifted on the crate. 'I could always take you for a drive. You'd look pretty in my soft top. I'll take you to Hereford to eat strawberries.' Ruth giggled. 'I'm serious doll,' Gina said. 'Fancy it?'

'Hereford? Why?'

'Strawberries! My cousin's got a vegetarian café there. She's got three specialities, right? Pumpkin, leek and strawberries. It's hot innit? She'll be doin' all sorts of shit wiv strawberries; tarts and ice-cream and fuckin' strawberries in lemon sauce.'

'You don't seem like the kind of woman who appreciates strawberries.'

'Yeah I know, but *you* do.'

'I don't though,' Ruth said. 'I don't like straw –'

The car slid calmly into the court, a lime green Ford Capri, a C Reg 1.6 Laser. It stopped beside the women, its engine still running. Ruth could grasp the traits of a personality by looking at the car a man bought. The domesticated types drove saloons and estates, cars with space to accommodate their kid's BMX. The sports cars, the spiders and spitfires were playboy's pussy wagons. But cars, like jewellery, were deceptive. If you were looking for riches you may as well start with a Fiat. Most of the BMW's you saw cruising the main roads of the Valleys were paid for with ball-breaking APR. After eighteen years in manufacture the last Capri rolled off the production line in December '86. In the summer of '91 it was awkward to know if its owner was just trying to be ironic. But she *felt* as though he was a loser; it was probably the spray job.

'You open?' he said.

Gina grimaced and shrugged her shoulders.

'Yeah we're open.' Ruth stood up, kicking her milk crate skidding across the court.

'Yeah, we're open,' Gina said, mimicking her zeal.

The man got out of the car. He was wearing a black leather jacket trimmed with fringes and nickel nipple shields. Ruth stood rigid in the centre of the yard, the aluminium Coke can crumpling in her wet fist. It was Simon's jacket.

'It's the brake pads,' he said. He slammed the door. Ruth visually measured the distance to the entrance of the garden centre. But it was too late to run. She watched his balding head twist around to face her. His features turned bombastic with excitement, like a child at the front of a roller coaster queue.

'Ruth –' he said.

'Simon,' she said. 'I didn't know you got your licence.'

'I haven't seen you for years. I've got lots of things,' he said. 'Is this where you work?'

'Brake pads'll take about an hour.' Ruth was trembling but her voice was bold and concise. 'You'll want to come back at quarter to four.'

'Can I wait?'

Gina was quizzically watching the exchange, still perched on the computer chair. 'You two know each ovver?' she said.

'Since school,' he said.

Gina frowned at Simon. 'Gimme the keys,' she said. 'I'll do it. Take your school friend here to Stuff Your Cakehole on the High Street. Buy her somefin' wiv strawberry in it.'

'Stuff Your Cakehole?' Simon said, grinning, his cheeks swollen with glee.

'Gina!' Ruth said. 'I can't go –'

'Stuff Your Cakehole,' Gina said, pointing past the roundabout towards town, 'or I'll fuckin' fire you. How'd you like that?'

The heat was constricting. Ruth walked ahead of Simon, her organs pumping and deafening her. She passed the music from the park, hearing only the stomp of her Dr Marten soles on the pavement. Pigeons flicked fag butts around the precinct with their scabby beaks. The gaggle disbanded as she filed through. At the dry fountain on the island, the idle road widened. Simon walked beside her.

'Is this where you've been all the time?' he said. 'Ponty? Working for that bitch?'

Ruth didn't look up from her toecaps. 'Now you've found me,' she said. 'How many attempts before you passed?'

'What?'

'Your test?'

'Four,' he said. He stopped and looked around at the High Street. 'Where are you going? That cake shop is over there.' Ruth looked at him, glaring at the cake shop through his thick, old fashioned spectacles. Underneath his coat his skin must have been weeping. Ruth's own skin flushed with the cogent image.

'The pub,' she said. She marched along the cobbles towards the Market Tavern. She knew that Gina used to work the streets of Manchester with a can of mace in her lace suspender belt. Her pimp let her keep enough money for a meal every week. The trick, she said, to surviving difficult situations, is simply to keep breathing. 'Like the Bee Gee's song, just *staying alive.*'

In the lounge, dust motes settled on Sunday lunch. The sweet odour of alcohol was intoxicating. Behind the bar, Ian smiled easily at her, wiping his hands on his white pinafore. His emerald colour eyes caught the rays coming through the net curtains. She ordered Mexican Corona.

'Take your overalls off at the table, Roo,' he whispered. 'Garfield's here cooking the books.' He put the bottle down gently on the towel in front of her and looked grudgingly at Simon.

'Best not,' Simon said, 'driving.' He curled his fingers around an imaginary steering wheel, snickering self consciously. 'Glass of lemonade.'

Ian smoothed his fingers into his black hair while he aimed the pump into the glass. The liquid gushed portentously. Simon's nostrils flared open as though he could smell something spiteful. Ruth sighed and walked to a table. She sat with her back to the window, wriggling out of the ripped torso of her overall. She tied the empty sleeves around her waist.

'So what's new?' Simon said, approaching.

In 1984, Ruth had been seventeen. There was an end of term party at Benny's house, on the estate. Leah'd stolen rum from her father's cabinet. They were drinking it with blackcurrant in his damp and smoky bedroom. She remembered her stripy tights splayed over the Star Wars duvet. On the stained carpet beneath her, her classmates were spinning a wine bottle. Simon didn't go to her comprehensive. He went on the blue bus to the Church school in the opposite valley. His parents were born again. But he was at the party, on the bed next to her. In the morning she woke early to the smell of vomit. Leah was on the floor with Benny, giggling. Ruth's fully clothed body was hot and numb. Very steadily she realised that Simon's dead arm was locked around her neck. That's how he came into her life.

The unreciprocated desire which had chased her for eight years began there, on a teenager's sticky quilt. She'd flinched as she watched Benny lick Leah's ears. She ached to be on the carpet with him, the platinum blonde punk with a guitar and a boa constrictor. He was Blaencwm's answer to Billy Idol. At school her stomach swam deliciously when he carved Anarchy symbols in her text book covers. But Benny never really cared for Ruth. She was already working at night in the garage with all of her brothers, panel beating and earning a small wage. You'd think she'd have a queue of adolescent men lining up to get a slice, their facial hair blunt from unnecessary shaves. Meat Loaf was on the radio singing about Modern Girls, but it was the same as ever. Boys asked her to fix their bike chains but never asked her out, because there is seemingly something fundamentally wrong with a woman who can carry more bacon home than her spouse. Simon spent his evenings alone playing electronic tennis on his BBC computer, a geek with no interest in the photographs of blood red Ferraris on Benny's wall. He had no interest in knowing how to start one, let alone knowing how its engine functioned. Some people were born to use buses and Simon was one of them. Mechanics could have been as feminine an activity, in his mind, as baking a fairy cake. She pushed his heavy arm off her but he groaned and brought it back like a guillotine. For a minute they thrust it back and forth, like a seesaw of flesh. She didn't know then that it would always be this way. It would take another five years before she snapped.

He was at her flat on the night before she ran away.

'Are you going out tonight?' he said. 'Or are you putting make-up on for fun?'

'Nail polish is hardly make-up, Sime.'

'Well,' he said puffing, 'technically it is.'

Ruth looked at him sitting in her armchair in his fringed jacket. Wisps of hair sprouted out of the neckline.

'No, I'm staying in,' she said. 'I'm tired.' It was a lie when she said it but as soon as her words were out, it was true, her energy sapped just with having to say it. She was tired of sitting in the bar next to him, everyone thinking that they were together. All her fledgling relationships had been ruined by his omnipresence. She leant down and continued coating her toes with the cerise varnish. He helped himself to her cigarettes. Outside the orange lamp-lights flickered on. Over small distances she heard glass smashing against walls. Young adults' neurotic screams arced into the night; lack of or over indulgence in narcotics – the village had gone to the dogs.

'I really am tired,' she said. 'I need to get an early night.'

'Don't mind me,' he said. 'I know my way around.'

She sat for a moment longer, considering shrieking, like the junkies outside. 'I hate you,' she wanted to say. The words were wobbling like boiled sweets on the edge of her tongue. She'd never really learned how to handle men. She flirted with her customers, swindled them, measured them, but she'd done it all for profit. Simon had ensured that she never really got around to learning about real emotions. Now it was time to tell him that she didn't want

167

him, to let him down gently, but he was paranoid and insecure and she simply didn't possess the skills. Many times she thought about asking her brothers to speak to him, but they'd say what they always said. 'We never wanted a girl working here. We never taught you how to service a car, you taught yourself. You can fight your own battles, tomboy.'

'Just give him the sympathy fuck,' Leah'd said when they were twenty. 'He'll probably disappear.' She never did, she knew Leah underestimated his fervour. Nobody had loved Leah like Simon loved Ruth. Benny'd left her for her little sister.

Ruth was lying in bed listening to her microwave heating her food. The sound was keeping her awake, sick, and thinking about cleaning because he'd been inside the house. Moments later he came to the bedroom.

'I'll sleep on the floor in here Ruth,' he said. 'It's cold out there.' He made himself comfortable on her goat skin rug. If people moved quickly enough, even in their most obscene actions, they could make it appear natural. It was like a mother getting attacked on a rush hour tube station, or burglars emptying a house in two minutes flat. She hugged the hemline of her nightdress tightly around her legs when she stepped over him to flick off the light. As Simon began to snore, she sobbed. Her life was miserable. She spent her leisure time collecting information on perfect contract killings, a chess piece for an evil fairy to move around. There, next to him, it seemed plain that he was stalking her, blatantly opening the door instead of peering through the letterbox, and running was her only option.

Customers were leaving the pub. Ian collected glasses, often floating near the table in earshot of conversational strands. Simon fidgeted and frowned at him sideways. 'Why didn't you tell me that this is where you were?' he said. 'I've been here thousands of times, I could have passed you on the street.'

Ruth stared at the surface of the table. In all the months he'd had to consider her retrospectively, it never crossed his mind that she was hiding from him. He had never questioned it. She'd worried her brothers and longed to see their laughing faces, but for nothing. 'What's the time?' she said. 'Is it time to go yet?'

She couldn't look at Ian, although she felt his confused gaze on her shoulders. Whatever was about to happen between them was probably over now.

'Ruth, the garage is this way,' Simon said.

'Yeah I know where it is,' she said. 'I'm going home. You heard her, she's sacking me anyway.'

'But I need to get the car.' He looked up and down the high street like a kid trying to cross the road. 'I'll visit you in the week,' he said. Ruth was already walking.

The sun shone again on Monday. Ruth plugged her earphones into her lugs, hurrying away from her three storey on Broadway. An elderly woman said something to her but Ruth faked a smile and turned away. She'd smelled of urine. Near the job centre she stopped to listen to the news. 'A twenty-six year old man died in a collision on a slip road near Pontypridd last night,' the reader was saying. It was a woman's voice laced with honey and pity.

'He'd been driving a Ford Capri.' She felt her fingernails cut into her palms.

'You're early,' Gina said, 'and white as a ghost.'

'Yeah, and you.'

'Police have been, doll, that mate of yours popped his clogs.'

'I know, what did you do?'

Gina pressed her hand on Ruth's shoulder. 'Me?' she said. 'He was driving a Capri, doll. I did the pads but he didn't say anything about the rubbers, probably perished, can't hold the fluid, a particular fault. Ruth, you should know this.'

'What did they say? The coppers?'

'Nothing, it was routine. I told them, particular fault, they're checking it out.'

'He said he was coming back in the week.'

'I know, babe,' Gina said. She rubbed Ruth's back with her clumsy, fatty hand. She'd never burped a baby. 'He's not though, doll. He's dead.'

Acknowledgements

Acknowledgements are due to the following magazines and anthologies in which some of the short stories in this collection first appeared: *Big Issue Cymru*; *New Welsh Review*; *Red Handed Magazine*; *Wales, Half Welsh* (Bloomsbury, 2004) and *Urban Welsh* (Parthian, 2005).

Jigsaws was written for the project Scritture Giovani 2002, promoted by Festivaletteratura Mantova, The Guardian Hay Festival and Internationales Literaturfestival Berlin, with funding from the European Community.

Thanks are also due to the following for their advice, support and generosity: Rajeev Balasbrumanyam, Lyndy Cooke, Gwen Davies, Lewis Davies, Peter Florence, Hannah Griffiths and Francesca Rhydderch. Also, a very special thanks to John Williams who commissioned and edited many of these stories before a collection was ever dreamt up.